SOLD

What will it take to find freedom?

Sue Barrow

cadence

Copyright © 2022 by Sue Barrow

Reprinted 2023

All rights reserved.

No portion of this book may be reproduced in any form without written permission from the publisher or author, except as permitted by UK copyright law.

ISBN 978-1-914578-08-3 (UK paperback)

ISBN 978-1-914578-02-1 (Hardback)

ISBN 978-1-914578-01-4 (E-book)

ISBN 978-1-914578-00-7 (POD paperback)

This is a work of fiction. Names, characters, places and incidents are the product of the author's imagination, or are used fictitiously. Any resemblance to actual persons, living or dead, is entirely coincidental.

Cover design by Jennette Slade

Printed and bound in Great Britain by Clays Ltd, Elcograf SpA

Published by Cadence Publishing – www.cadencepublishing.com

For the young women I have had the privilege of spending time with, who have endured and survived trafficking and shared their own stories with me –
  this book is dedicated to them.

Chapter One

A village in Albania: 26th February

ROZA TAPPED HER FOOT on the classroom floor. Mrs Cicu had asked her to stay behind and now it was after four. Mami would be expecting her home. Ylli waiting at the window, clutching the sticks he and Roza had gathered, ready to toss them under the bridge and scream with excitement as they reappeared on the other side.

Mrs Cicu was pinning something to the wall. A painting. 'Something light to discuss after prize-giving tomorrow, I think.'

Roza smiled and moved a step closer. The picture was pulling her in like a magnet.

A smoggy harbour. Stick figures in a rowboat. Corkscrews of orange sunlight dancing over the smooth, still water.

'So, you like Monet's *Sunrise*!' Her teacher's face lit up with approval.

Like? Couldn't she hear her heart hammering? It was as if Mr Monet was trying to tell her about a future that was different, something new and exciting springing up, the darkness of the past year fading away.

Mrs Cicu reached into her coat pocket. There was a moment's hesitation before she held out a small square of card. 'My sister Juliana's husband. He is a journalist; a very good man. If ever you should be in need . . .'

Roza was barely listening. She skimmed the words. A name and address in London.

That was strange. *Monet*. Did they really share the same name, this artist and Mrs Cicu's brother-in-law?

'Here, help me carry these out, would you?' Her teacher slid her hands under a stack of exercise books.

Outside it looked like rain. Thunder grumbled faintly in the distance. Ylli wouldn't get his walk after all.

Roza turned at the door. One last look at the painting for now. She'd see it again tomorrow.

She walked with Mrs Cicu towards her car.

'You'd better hurry home, Roza. Sounds like a storm brewing.' A wisp of Mrs Cicu's dark hair had come loose in the wind. She tucked it into her bun and slipped into the driving seat. 'I'll see you in the morning. Don't be late for prize-giving.

'And Roza . . .' She nodded at the card still in the girl's hand. 'Don't forget! Things aren't always as they seem.'

Roza heaved a sigh as the rain splattered on to the card, blurring the letters. Mrs Cicu hadn't had one positive thing to say about Roza going to the UK. Her cousins were offering her a new home, she had been specially chosen, everything would be provided. Nothing ambiguous about that.

Her mouth stretched into a smug smile. Mrs Cicu was kind, and an excellent teacher, but she did not know everything.

Roza tore the card into tiny pieces. Then lifted her head and watched as the wind whipped them high into the air, scattering them like wedding confetti.

Chapter Two

27th February

FLIGHT 4102 HEAVED ITS way across the night sky like a monster under attack.

'No cause for concern, ladies and gentlemen, but I'm afraid we've hit a patch of bad weather.'

The pilot's voice sounded far too jovial for Roza's liking. The plane juddered as though it agreed with her. Jagged slashes of lightning brightened the blackness like fireworks on Independence Day. Hailstones beat against the window. She gripped the arms of her seat. *No cause for concern?* It looked like the end of the world to her.

As the turbulence settled, she forced her eyes back to the screen. A horse was galloping across a First World War landscape, nostrils flaring. But Roza couldn't concentrate. The whole day had been bizarre.

She'd missed prize-giving and the chance to say good-bye to her mother and brothers. And then, at the airport, Aunty Sade, who should have been seeing her off, had abandoned her.

One minute she'd been firing instructions into her phone about a delivery of *cargo*, (whatever that meant); the next, she was gathering her things together with such haste Roza found herself looking around for the fire. Aunty hadn't even said a proper goodbye. Just, 'Dori will see you on to the plane.' And that in a snappy sort of voice.

Dori. As Roza closed her eyes, the woman's face loomed up at her – tight-jawed, eyes flashing, her liver-spotted hand coming down hard on the baby's leg in the airport rest room. And *this* was the woman who was supposed to be looking after her? Well, if the way she was treating her own flesh and blood was anything to go by, Roza would take her chances alone.

She straightened her spine to peer over the seats in front. It wasn't easy to pick someone out by the back of their head, especially someone as short as Dori. Then she spied the collar of her dark mac.

The woman flexed her neck from side to side. The next moment she was up on her feet, dumping the baby on the older girl in the seat beside her and smoothing down her lemon two-piece. Swaying up the aisle towards Roza she looked like a sweet grandmother with her soft powdered cheeks and permed grey hair.

She leaned across the empty seat.

A chain bracelet decorated with twin-headed snakes dangled in Roza's face.

'Enjoying the flight?' Her voice was high and husky as though she had a cold. 'There is a free seat near us. Bring your case with you.'

'No!' Roza shifted uncomfortably. 'I . . . I'd prefer to stay here, thank you.'

'Your aunty asked me to look after you.' Dori spoke through gritted teeth.

'I like this seat. I can look out of the window.' Roza turned her back.

'Is anything wrong?' The steward balancing a tray of drinks angled his head.

Roza forced a smile. 'I'm fine. Thank you.'

With that, Dori left.

Roza watched as the steward delivered the tall glasses filled with something fizzy, without spilling a drop. She couldn't afford to attract any attention. If anyone looked too closely at her, they might ask other questions.

She looked down at the hideous outfit Aunty Sade had produced for her to wear for the journey. A black skirt that came down to her calves and maroon blouse with a pussy bow. Something Aunty would wear, not a young girl.

Roza pulled out her passport and studied the name and age underneath her photo. Three weeks before, her father had taken her to the local registry office. She had to sit on a revolving stool inside a curtained booth while the camera clicked in rapid succession. *One, two, three.* It had happened so quickly she was afraid her eyes would be shut in every photo. When they slipped out shiny and damp it was a nice surprise. She looked older somehow – her straight mousy hair combed around her face instead of tied back with her usual bobble. She couldn't do anything about her snub nose but the little bit of eye shadow Aunty had suggested emphasised the shape of her grey eyes.

'When you travel you must look smart and . . .' Babi had faltered. 'Sophisticated, yes.'

It wasn't a Babi word. Had Aunty told him to say that? Just as she had told Roza today that the name on her travel documents had been changed?

'It is better that in Britain you are known by the name of my daughter's husband.' Aunty had spelled it out – *Braka* - as they queued for the car park.

Roza tried it out in her head. All those hard consonants, she didn't like it at all. Her name was Roza Noli.

Aunty Sade's red mouth turned up at the corners again. 'And there is something else.'

'I know.' Roza's shoulders sagged. 'Babi told me I am to call my cousins Aunty and Uncle.'

'In private, yes, but if anyone asks, they are your parents. It is less complicated that way.'

Roza opened her mouth to ask about the date of birth. It made her nearly seventeen when actually she wouldn't be fifteen until April.

'And Roza . . . do not ask so many questions. It is a bad habit of yours.'

Another heavy squall pounded the plane. A collective gasp went up as it juddered and tipped to one side.

Deep breaths. Everything would be OK.

Flying to the UK was the beginning of a big adventure. A new school, new clothes and – she felt a stab of guilt admitting it – an escape from all the drudgery at home. *The opportunity of a lifetime* Babi had called it. The words warmed her as she let them roll around her head. Her shoulders loosened. Tomorrow these minor glitches would all be behind her. And she would never have to look that Dori woman in the face again.

Roza reached into her backpack and felt for the scrap she had torn off the raggedy blanket her little brother took to bed with him each night. She might have missed the chance to say goodbye but a little bit of Ylli was coming to the UK with her.

The buffeting eased. Runway lights radiated against a grubby February sky. Dots of light spread into splashes. The plane swooped lower and lower then hit the ground with a jolt.

Suddenly everyone was on their feet, stretching and smiling as though they knew all along everything would come right.

Roza pulled her backpack between her shoulders and joined the line to the exit.

'Travelling alone?'

The florid-faced man at the immigration desk held up her passport. His eyes flicked between the photo and the real her. Perhaps she didn't look so sophisticated after all. 'Someone meeting you?'

'My . . . uncle, sir.'

The hesitation on his face made Roza think there was a question coming.

A broad-chested man with a thick moustache joined him in the booth. 'Excuse me, Harry. Can I interrupt you for a minute?'

With barely another glance at Roza, the man with the red face brought his stamp down hard on her passport. 'Move on,' he said.

Immigration, baggage, customs.

Roza followed her best friend's advice about weaving her way to the edge of the luggage carousel. 'Excuse me. Sorry.' She straightened her backpack – Stefanie's leaving gift – with its elephant motif and red vertical stripes.

Elephants never forget! And don't you forget me, Roza Noli!

Roza smiled. She had no intention of forgetting her friend or – virtual eye roll – her request for a postcard of Buckingham Palace.

Fifteen minutes later she was marching towards the exit sign. Roza fell into step alongside twin boys weighed down by bulging rucksacks. She exchanged shy smiles with the one next to her, wishing for a second that she was going home with them, not the stranger who would be meeting her. For all her instructions, Aunty hadn't thought to give her a photo of Uncle Jozif. How would she know it was him?

She battled her way through the tangle of reunion celebrations, the shiny *Welcome Home* balloons and the ragged line of people holding up name cards.

Her name wasn't among them. Had Uncle Jozif been held up? Was there some confusion about the time?

Roza found a gap against the wall and slid on to the floor. Weariness washed over her like a wave of cold water. She buried her head between her knees. All she wanted at this moment was her lumpy bed at home and little Ylli's warm body cuddled into hers.

As she looked up, a stocky man was hurrying towards her in a flat-footed kind of way, clutching a card to his hip as though he was too self-conscious to hold it up. Roza tilted her head to read the slanting letters. *BRAKA*. She almost looked away and then remembered it was supposed to be *her* name.

'You are Roza?' She supposed this was Uncle Jozif. He gave her an odd look, as though she wasn't what he was expecting, and picked up her case with its wonky handle and dog-eared corners. 'Follow me,' he said.

Before she knew it, they were stepping out of lift doors into a car park. Cold air swirled around, lifting Roza's skirt. The wind had driven the rain in and she had to keep her eyes down, concentrating on stepping between the puddles to keep her shoes dry. She didn't see the blue hatchback shooting towards them.

Uncle flung an arm out to protect her.

'Damn fool!' The car screeched to a stop and he rapped the side window.

A flash of silver caught Roza's eye as the driver waggled the gear stick.

It was *her* – Dori. But where were her grandchildren? The back seat was empty.

Chapter Three

Thornley Combe

'ARE YOU HUNGRY?'

They had been driving for almost an hour when Uncle Jozif pulled on to a garage forecourt. Head down, he ran through the rain to the cabin and returned with sandwiches in a plastic packet and a can of cola.

She thanked him in the Albanian he had been speaking. She hoped there would be more English spoken when they arrived at her new home but right now it was more effort than she could be bothered with.

Uncle Jozif drove away and accelerated into a bend. Water flooded across the windscreen. He grunted with amusement as Roza gripped the door handle. 'You're not used to fast cars?' he said.

'My father's car is quite old,' she replied, covering her mouth to disguise a burp. The chicken sandwiches were very spicy. 'Lorik drove a motorbike for a while but...'

'You have a brother?'

'One older, one younger.'

And a sister. But she died last August.

She wasn't going to tell him about Sindi. Even now, six months on, thinking about it made her throat close up. She drained the last of the cola and gave in to the heaviness tugging at her eyelids.

When she woke an hour later, they were sitting at traffic lights. Her eyes flitted between the shops, their windows lit up on either side of the road. *Peacocks, Gregg's, Tammy's Takeaway.* Roza wiped the string of dribble from her chin. 'What is the name of this place, sir?'

'Thornley Combe. In Oxfordshire.'

'Near the Oxford university?' Elegant spires and towers, dons in their black academic gowns, students punting on the river – Roza had seen plenty of photos on Mrs Cicu's computer.

'Not really,' he said.

'But can we go there one day? It would be a dream come true for me.'

Uncle wasn't interested in her dreams. In a droning voice he explained how Thornley was a new place for his family, that he was a doctor at the nearby health centre and his wife worked at the council offices.

'Adelina and the boys, they should have moved in today from our former home in Brighton. But the storms. As you see, there has been some flooding. The furniture will arrive ahead of my wife the day after tomorrow.' The lights turned green and he pulled away. 'You will have to sleep on the floor tonight.'

Roza said nothing. Where did he think she slept when *Gjyshe* came to stay?

The lamp-lit roads narrowed. Some of the houses were taller than any building in her village. There were lots of shiny cars, at least one in every driveway. Uncle swung on to a slab of tarmac and jerked up the handbrake. Stretching his arms, he let out a full-throated yawn. His breath smelled sour.

'You can get out. I'll bring your case.' He paused, his hand on the open door. 'And er . . . let me have your passport, for safekeeping.'

Behind the front door there was a pile of mail. Roza waited for Uncle to pick it up before following him inside. Instinctively, she slipped off her shoes. She turned full circle. This wasn't a house; it was a mansion! Bigger even than Aunty Sade's. The hallway here was almost the size of their whole house with four, no five, doors leading off it. And – she glanced up – a chandelier, twinkling like a galaxy of stars.

At home, all they had was a room where Babi and Mami slept and a cubbyhole bed under the eaves she shared with Ylli. Lorik had to manage on a mattress put down in the living room every night. Apart from the tiny kitchen at the back that was it.

Roza hugged herself. Was she really going to live here?

'Bathroom is across the landing.' Uncle was halfway up the stairs. His voice echoed as he dumped her suitcase in an empty room at the back and unrolled a mattress no thicker than her school exercise book. She wiggled her toes, letting them sink deep into the soft cream carpet.

'Naten e mire,' *Goodnight,* she whispered to his back as he pulled the door behind him.

Roza burrowed under the blankets, pulling her knees into her chest as she began a thank-you prayer for her new family. She paused. Uncle's voice was seeping through the wall. And with a sharpness to it she hadn't expected.

'Yes, yes, of course. No, I have taken care of that.'

Roza covered her ears. She shouldn't be eavesdropping. Where had she got to? Oh yes . . . Jozif, Adelina, Skender, Albi. Theirs were the names on her lips as she drifted into sleep.

***

'We will buy only essentials,' Uncle said as they drove to the supermarket the next morning.

The early start had come as a shock. He had barely given Roza time to shower. But it was a bright day. Even the puddles sparkled.

'This place seems so friendly.' She smiled at a pair of old ladies in checked coats and soft hats chatting at the pedestrian crossing. 'So much nicer than where I come from.'

Children begging on the streets. Roads pitted with potholes and no wider than farm tracks. Last month, a neighbour three doors down had been shot by men burgling his house.

Uncle parked up and led the way across the car park. Roza's conscience pricked her. Not everything at home was bad. She had parents who loved her, a teacher who gave her extra English lessons for free.

The sign over the supermarket entrance stopped her in her tracks. 'More than forty thousand items for sale? Can that really be true, sir?'

Uncle went ahead, pushing a trolley.

At home they ate the same food most weeks – beans, leftover vegetables and cheap cuts from the butcher that no one else wanted. Even the nearest supermarket, more than ten miles away, was nothing like this.

Roza trailed behind him, examining the labels. Chunky fillets of chicken and steak, wafer thin slices of meat – salami, pastrami, prosciutto. She was struggling to get her tongue around the unfamiliar words when at last she found something she recognised.

'Pizza! And look, so many flavours – ham, pineapple, chorizo sausage . . .'

She snatched one up, remembering the first time she had tasted pizza at Mrs Cicu's. Her husband had brought one back from a trip to Tirana. Roza hadn't stopped talking about it for days, much to Babi's annoyance.

Now Uncle looked impatient. She must be talking too much. Roza clamped her lips together and hurried after him. When he stopped to pull a blue checked shirt down from a rail and held it against his large stomach she spotted rails of girls' clothes further along. And all brand new. Not like the tops and trousers Mami had to sort through at the second-hand market.

Roza made a mental note of the items she would need. Aunty would be sure to ask her. She stroked the pile on a long jacket with deep pockets and fleecy cuffs. A warm coat would be top of the list.

Only one more thing would make the day perfect.

Uncle had taken a different turning out of the car park. She squeezed her fists under her chin as they passed a cinema on one side and a couple of smart restaurants on the other. They were heading towards a stretch of green where boys in striped jerseys were chasing a football around. Beyond it, an immense, dark stone building that looked as though it had stood there for hundreds of years. A sign flashed by. She was right!

Roza splayed her fingers against the glass. 'That is it, isn't it? My new school?' She swung around. 'When will I start, sir?

'You will have to ask my wife,' he said, his eyes fixed to the windscreen. 'I don't know what her plans are.'

As soon as they were back, Roza slipped upstairs to the bedroom she was sure would be hers.

Now she was not rushing anywhere, she noticed properly the wall covering – the raised splashes of pink, like strawberries. Uncle had told her the people who lived here before had a daughter about her age. Sitting cross-legged on her bedroll, she pictured the furniture she would like. A chest of drawers for her new clothes (obviously), a desk under the window where she could do her homework. A mirror, certainly. And something for the wall? A copy of that painting Mrs Cicu had shown her, perhaps. She'd ask Uncle if she could buy a copy online when his computer arrived with the rest of the furniture.

Her own room! Something she could never have hoped for at home. And with a view of the garden – wide strips of grass, daffodils lining a paved path, a wooden door at the end painted green.

If Sindi had lived Ylli would have moved downstairs with Lorik, leaving the two girls to share the roof space. Roza pulled out the family photo she had snuck into her backpack and looked into the baby's face. Six months ago tomorrow . . .

Sindi had arrived two days after Easter, when Mami's due date was still six weeks away. Her cries were thin and reedy as though she knew it was too soon to leave Mami's womb.

As usual, Aunty Sade didn't waste any time voicing her opinion.

'A boy with strong arms and legs would have been more use.'

Roza rolled her eyes as far as they would go. She was fond of her big brother but the last thing their family needed was another son like Lorik. Spending half his day repairing TV sets for Mr Napoleon and the other half stealing motorbikes and chasing girls.

At four months, Sindi's arms and legs were still stick-thin. Worse, she developed a cough and a fever that wouldn't go away. Mami wanted to take her to the local health centre.

'Doctors? Medicines?' Babi's face assumed the look of panic it always did when money was needed. Treatment was supposed to be free but everyone knew under-the-counter payments were expected.

'The oldest two grew up healthy enough without the need for needles and drugs,' he added.

'For God's sake, Arben, ask your sister for the money!' Sindi was swaddled against Mami, grizzling, her fuzzy cap of hair wet from the fever.

It cost Mami a lot to make that request. Aunty had never forgiven her for getting in the family way before she and Babi were married. *Entrapment* she called it, giving her r's an extra roll.

Whether Babi spoke to Aunty Sade or not, it made no difference. By the time Sindi saw a doctor, the infection was in her blood. She died a week later.

Their family had never been the same since. It started to unravel, like a ball of string.

Roza stood up and stretched her arms high above her head. She was here now. Free to leave all that sadness behind.

Downstairs, Uncle was in the garage checking whether the previous tenants had left anything behind.

Roza circled the kitchen, fingering each appliance, running her hands along the smooth, hard surfaces. It was amazing how everything fitted and matched and responded to the touch of a button or the flick of a switch. The way water gushed out hot and cold from the same tap.

At the far end, she found another toilet with a small sink. Opposite, a door which was narrower than all the others in the house. Roza flicked the light switch on the wall outside. The room was barely longer than her own body and the only daylight came from a small window with thick patterned glass. Two machines stood beneath it – each with a concave door and a dial.

A box of washing powder sat on top of one. A laundry room, of course, much like the one in Stefanie's house.

Later, she and Uncle prepared supper together and he showed her how to use the tin opener. After dumping the fried sausages on to paper plates, he poured boiling water into a round glass bowl half-filled with white granules.

'Potato out of a packet!' Roza exclaimed as he mixed it vigorously, splattering lumps over the side.

She lifted a forkful to her mouth as Uncle slurped tomato ketchup over his meal. 'I will be very happy to help with preparing meals. I am used . . . *was* used,' she corrected herself with a short laugh, 'to cooking at home. Some digging in the garden as well if someone will show me what to do. Mami had a vegetable patch until . . .'

She stopped and looked up. Uncle was pulling slice after slice of bread from the packet, mopping up the sauce with slow circular movements. He had barely raised his eyes from his newspaper since he sat down.

'I have unpacked my case and put my clothes away in the cupboard. In the bedroom where I slept last night. I hope that was all right.' The words tumbled out in a rush.

Uncle scraped his chair back and pushed his leftovers into the bin. When he lifted his head, the reluctance on his face told her exactly what he was going to say.

'You will have to ask my wife about that.'

Chapter Four

THE NEXT MORNING A removal van pulled up outside before it was properly light.

Roza stumbled on to the landing and peered down the stairwell to find her uncle still in his vest and shorts. A dark shadow of stubble stained his chin. He pressed himself against the wall as two men in dark blue overalls began spreading plastic sheeting across the hall and up the stairs.

'They are early! You must help me find Adelina's list.'

Roza tugged her nightdress down as far as it would go. Babi had a habit of mislaying things at the garage – invoices for repairs, order sheets. She often found them for him in the most unexpected places. When she suggested the car, Uncle slapped his head with the palm of his hand, ran down the steps and produced it from the glove box at the front.

'Everything must be in order by the time my wife arrives. *Everything*. Adelina was most insistent her instructions be followed to the letter.' As if it was burning his fingers, he thrust the list into Roza's hand.

Capital letters and exclamation marks jumped out at her:
CHECK SHOES BEFORE MEN GO UPSTAIRS!
MAKE SURE FURNITURE PLACED IN THE RIGHT ROOMS

EXAMINE THE GLASSES AND CHINA BEFORE THEY LEAVE!

Roza flipped it over and back again. There were plenty of references to the boys' bedrooms but nothing about her own.

'Upstairs, Roza! No time to waste. Take the list with you.'

It was hard physical work and certainly not the way Roza had expected to spend her second day. But as the hours passed, something inside her lifted. She was playing her part in building their new home, like one of the family.

'I hope Aunty will be pleased with our efforts,' she said brightly, following her uncle around the house with his toolbox, helping him hang one mirror after another.

Only one thing spoiled it. Roza had lost count of the number of times Uncle Jozif's phone buzzed like an angry wasp. *Aunt Adelina? Again?* Surely she would be pleased when she saw the progress they had made, and in such a short time? Unpacking the china and putting it through the dishwasher – even hanging curtains in the front room.

It was growing dark by the time headlamps bounced up the drive announcing Aunt Adelina's arrival. Roza and Uncle had been in the garage stuffing furniture packaging into recycling bags long enough that her hands were stiff and icy.

At first, all Roza could see was Adelina's back and the row of slim gold bangles that jangled up and down her arm as she leaned in to unbuckle the little boy from his seat.

'Is anyone going to help me here?' She spun round with such a cross face that Roza shrank back inside the garage.

She had fat arms and short legs. Her black hair was cropped short in jagged spikes and she was dressed from head to toe in the same shade: tight-fitting jeans, a sweater which rode up to reveal a girdle of fat, and spiky-heeled ankle boots.

Jozif wiped his hands on his trousers and hurried forward, his face wreathed in smiles. 'Hello, Albi.' The little boy raced up to him and wrapped his arms around one of Jozif's legs. A floppy kangaroo hung from his hand. He was chubbier than Ylli but with his white-blond hair and green eyes the likeness was striking.

The older boy – Skender – remained in the car. Wires hung from his ears and his feet dangled over the front seat either side of a small TV screen. Roza tried to size him up without staring. With his long narrow face, he looked nothing like his younger brother. How old was he? Thirteen, fourteen at the most?

'Did you have a smooth trip, Adelina?' Jozif swung his son into his arms and stepped forward to plant a kiss on her cheek.

She swatted him away. 'Is everything in? I hope you've cleared up after them.' Adelina looked around. 'Where is the girl?'

Sucking in her breath, Roza stepped out of the shadows. *Eyes bright, chin up, best smile.* There was a little speech somewhere in her head, one she'd been piecing together all day, but the words wouldn't come. She smiled inanely.

'Humph! Scrawny, isn't she? I hope you've had her working.'

'We've made good progress indoors, as you will see.' Jozif deposited the little boy on the ground and, with a small bow, gestured towards the open front door.

Uncertain about following them inside Roza went back to the garage, hunching her shoulders against the cold. She picked up another carton. A street light at the foot of the drive gave out a dull yellow glow. Above it a sliver of moon.

Roza's chest ached. She and Babi always looked out for a new moon together, just as they had last month. As though it was some kind of talisman; something that might change their family's fortunes.

***

Babi had taken her with him to deliver a new car to one of his boss's best customers.

'Was Mr Miloti pleased with you, Babi?' Roza asked as they walked back home.

'For selling the Mercedes to Agim Krasniki?' Babi nodded. 'He has given me a share of the sale money.'

But his voice was flat.

Her father had gone into business with Stefanie's father, as his partner, when Roza was just a few months old and Lorik was three. Now Babi worked *for*, not *with* Mr Miloti. Roza was too young to know when this change took place but Lorik, who thought he knew everything, said Baba made some bad business decisions along the way and ever since had *paid the price*, whatever that meant.

Roza pointed upwards at the pale crescent rising early against the washed-out blue of the afternoon sky. That would raise a smile. 'A new moon, Babi.' She squeezed his arm. 'To confirm your good fortune.' There was a teasing note in her voice. She didn't believe today's success was linked to the moon any more than he did.

As they took the coast road home, Roza's heart lifted. Babi's mood had been so low lately but this felt special, just the two of them together. They walked and talked. Or rather *she* talked. About *Little Women*, the latest book Mrs Cicu had introduced her to. And the research she was doing on female equality to write her essay for prize-giving.

Roza waited for her father to say something. 'Is something wrong, Babi?'

Her father came to a halt. 'It's your mother.'

Roza looked at him in alarm. Mami hadn't been the same since Sindi had died. Was something seriously wrong and now he was going to break the bad news to her?

'She can no longer manage at home without you. Her *condition* . . .' Babi lowered his head. Roza looked away too. Sindi's birth had been difficult and had left Mami with *women's problems*. She rarely went out these days.

'She is going to need you at home more to look after Ylli.'

Not this again! Had Babi forgotten how much school she had missed in the past month looking after her brother and keeping house? It was only because she went to Mrs Cicu's two evenings a week after putting Ylli to bed that she was able to keep up with her studies.

'I'm afraid it means . . .'

Something clutched at Roza's chest. *No, don't say it!*

'You will have to leave school, Roza. It's not just your Mami; it is hard enough to find money for the bills every month, never mind the extra things you need – uniform, books . . .' His words tumbled out like they had been waiting a long time to be unlocked.

'Babi, please! I will work twice as hard at home . . .'

'I am sorry.' He shook his head. He truly was.

Can't Mami see a doctor? The words froze on her lips. Stupid question. Doctors cost money.

Babi reached for her hand but Roza snatched it away. Why had it never occurred to her that this might happen?

At last, Uncle was calling her name. She tied up the last bag of recycling and joined him at the front door. His face had a polished look from shaving and he had changed into suit trousers and a white shirt.

'I will gladly help prepare the evening meal,' Roza said brightly as she followed him into the hall.

'That will not be necessary. Wait here please.'

The kitchen door closed behind him with a soft thud. She slipped into the toilet. Perhaps Adelina had brought supper with her from *Tammy's Takeaway* and they were laying it out nicely to welcome her. Yes, that must be why Uncle had changed.

Roza dried her hands and stepped into the hall almost colliding with Skender and Albi. Like Jozif, they were dressed smartly – matching navy blue jackets, collared shirts and neck ties. The little one began playing hide-and-seek, weaving between the coats. Albi squealed as Skender made the stand rock from side to side.

Roza forced a smile.

'What does she have to look happy about?' Adelina planted herself in front of the mirror, gently pulling at spiny strands of hair.

Roza's eyes settled on Uncle Jozif who was swiping at a stripe of dust on his trousers. Surely he would break the silence with a light laugh and tell his wife that all day she had been helpful and hard-working.

'May I know . . . which is my bedroom?' Roza jumped in, her voice sounding high and unnatural. 'I . . . I would like to unpack later and . . .'

Adelina pouted at the mirror and applied a slick of red across her lips. 'Found your tongue, have you? You can begin with emptying the boys' cases and hanging their clothes in the wardrobes. After that, you will tidy the kitchen and make up the beds. There are sheets and blankets in each room.'

Albi wailed as Adelina gripped his arm to stop him diving back into the coats. 'Make sure you have finished by the time we get back.'

'*Get back?* I . . . I do not understand. Where . . . where are you *going*?'

Adelina shrugged her arms into the fake fur coat Jozif was holding open. 'That is no concern of *yours*. Your job is to stay here and follow my instructions.'

Her *job*! If Adelina had delivered a slap, Roza's cheeks couldn't have stung more.

She spun around. 'Uncle Jozif...?'

But he was already out through the door. He didn't even look back.

Chapter Five

No! TODAY WAS NOT supposed to end like this!

Roza folded an arm into her stomach and sank on to the stairs. She was not a crybaby and she would not give way to tears now. Her cousins wanted to share their good fortune with her, she had been *specially chosen*. Aunty Sade's exact words! This was a bad start. Nothing more.

Empty the cases. Make the beds. Rehearsing Adelina's instructions in her head she dragged her feet up the stairs. She might as well start in Albi's room. The room she had hoped would be *hers*. She wrestled a pillow into its cotton case and tucked in the sheets and blankets. Then she scanned the room. Her suitcase and backpack had been there earlier. Where were they now?

The wardrobe door was open. The clothes she had hung up had disappeared too. Instead, a black bag stuffed to the brim with girls' clothes – skirts, blouses, underwear, socks – was taking up the space next to Albi's t-shirts and trousers. Roza lifted out a purple sweatshirt and held it against her. With a frown, she folded it and put it back in the bag.

Next door, Skender's electronic gadgets littered the floor as though he had already tired of them. So this wasn't to be her room either. The locked door across the landing was Jozif and Adelina's bedroom. And she had already discounted the small

L-shaped room at the front where a computer and music system were waiting to be unpacked.

An uneasy feeling pressed down on Roza's chest. She didn't much care about her suitcase. And as far as she was concerned, the few clothes she had brought with her were destined for the bin. Her backpack was another matter. Along with the notebook and pencils Mrs Cicu had given her, there was Ylli's blanket scrap and the family photo she had lifted from its frame at the last minute. Babi's letter too – painstakingly written, thanking her cousins for the opportunity they were giving his daughter.

Roza pressed her hand against her chest. *Deep breaths.* There must be a simple explanation. She'd ask her cousin when the family returned.

Her stomach growled. Over six hours had passed since she and Jozif had shared a hurried lunch.

The loaf of bread was still on the kitchen counter, next to an open packet of cheese. She was trying hard not to think about the Brakas tucking into a full plate of food. Probably at one of the smart restaurants she and Uncle had passed yesterday.

Roza pulled out a slice of bread and spread it thickly with butter. As she bit into it, the doorbell chimed.

A pale shape shifted from side to side behind the frosted glass. Roza smoothed down her skirt and edged the door open. It was a woman wearing a pleated skirt and a green padded jacket, her hair shaped around her head like a coppery brown helmet. In her hands was a bunch of gaudy flowers.

'Good evening! Thought I'd pop over. Just to say hello.'

'Hello,' Roza said with a blank look

'Sorry, should have said. Pam Hardiman. Next door? Your parents out, are they?' Her staccato phrases jumped out in a rush. 'Leave these, shall I?'

People never called at home with flowers. What a kind gesture. 'No,

No . . . please, come in.'

Roza opened the door wide. At last, an opportunity to try out her English. 'Jerry's my other half,' Mrs Pam continued. 'You'll see him on his motorbike.

Hear him more like!'

'Our family is called Braka,' Roza said. 'Jozif and Adelina, and two boys – Skender and Albi.'

There, she had said it. Just as Aunty Sade told her to.

'And you, of course!'

'Yes. I am Roza.'

'Come far, have you? Nice neighbourhood this. Good schools. You'll be off to the Bishop I expect?'

So many questions. Now the woman was peering round the lounge door. Was she expecting a tour of the house?

'Um . . .' Roza took the flowers, cupping her hand under the wet stems. 'Thank you for these. I will put them in water.'

Mrs Pam sniffed. 'Tell your mother they're from the Hardimans. Just across the drive. Don't forget now.'

Roza closed the door behind her. Then she filled a jug and took her time arranging the stems. She placed it on the hall table. Adelina would see the flowers as soon as she walked in. It was only when she stepped back to admire her efforts that she noticed the light left on in the laundry room.

The door wouldn't open properly when she tried the handle. A mound of dirty clothes was in the way. She pushed harder and squeezed through the gap. The machines had been jammed closer together to make space for the old couch from the garage. She looked up. A screw had been driven through the handle that opened the tiny window.

A cold hollow feeling opened up inside her. The beads of sweat on his forehead, the dust on his trousers – Jozif must have moved the sofa before they went out. Was *this* where she was meant to sleep? *The laundry room?* Her foot struck something hard and she looked down. Her suitcase and backpack – they were poking out from under the couch.

Roza reached inside the pack. There was a secret pocket – Stefanie had been ridiculously excited to tell her that – so Ylli's corner of blanket was safe. But it was small comfort. Everything else was missing, even Babi's letter.

She wrapped her arms around her middle. Her whole body was trembling. She couldn't make it stop.

Stumbling into the living room she sank on to the sofa. Why were these awful things happening to her? She curled into a ball.

'Babi, what have you done?' she wailed.

'Who said you could come in here?'

Roza squinted up to find Adelina staring down at her. How long had she been sleeping? What time was it?

She cried out as Adelina dug her fingers into the fleshy bit at the top of her arm and dragged her into the hall.

'Where have these come from?' Adelina snatched the flowers out of the vase.

Roza tripped over her words as she explained about Mrs Pam.

'Nosy cow! Don't you dare let anyone in again.'

Roza's eyes travelled to the kitchen counter and her half-made sandwich. She hurried in to tidy the foodstuffs away.

'So you have been helping yourself? Repaying our kindness, by stealing from us?'

'No! I was hungry. I thought...'

'That you could come here and sponge off your relatives?'

The room was starting to sway. *Where was Uncle Jozif? Why was he letting his wife talk to her like this?*

Quickly, Roza tidied the counter. When she looked up, Adelina was standing outside the laundry room.

'You want to know which room is yours?' She held the door open.

'Please . . . no. I don't want to . . .'

'Don't just stand there. Get inside!'

Blackness descended as the key scraped in the lock behind her.

Roza felt her way to the small couch and lay down as best she could. Covering herself with the blanket, she stared into the darkness. What would the morning bring?

Chapter Six

A SOUND LIKE RAPID gunfire woke Roza with a jolt. No, that couldn't be right – she was in Oxfordshire. More likely, it was Mr Pam's motorbike.

She was desperate to pee. She tried the handle and the door gave way. Perhaps Uncle Jozif *had* said something to his wife.

Going to the loo was OK but splashing her face with cold water caused pain to pulse up her arm. A reminder, as if she needed one, of the night before. Was Adelina like that all the time?

Roza examined herself in the mirror. Today would be different. It was up to her to make it so; to be polite and obedient and helpful. *And* grateful. She shut her eyes, repeating the word to herself. Because she *was* grateful. A better life in the UK was what she had come for and if that meant she had to work a little harder to earn it, so be it. In spite of everything that had happened, she was certain that was what Babi would expect her to do.

She pulled a pair of dark trousers and a clean blouse from her case. Like most of what she'd brought, they were washed out and worn. But they would have to do until Adelina bought her something new.

She bundled the pile of dirty laundry from the floor into the washing machine. Mami always complained that their clothes were never properly clean because the water was not hot enough.

That wouldn't be a problem here. Roza turned the dial to the highest temperature – ninety degrees – and pressed the start button.

Footsteps padded in the hall. She darted into the kitchen.

'*Mirëmëngjes*. Good morning, Aunt Adelina.' Roza tried very hard not to stare at her. The woman was still in her nightclothes. Her early morning eyes were baggy and tufts of her hair were sticking up at odd angles.

'You stand there when I address you. And you call me Madam.'

Roza followed the direction of Adelina's finger to the mat by the back door. Any hope that the woman had woken in a kinder frame of mind was fading fast. She pulled a sheet of paper from her dressing gown pocket, one that was covered in dense, black writing.

'Every morning by this time you will have the breakfast laid out and the washing in the machine. Skender's lunch must be packed and in his bag before you take Albi to nursery. Everything you have to do is on this list. *Ever-y-thing*. Follow this and you will stay out of trouble. Is that clear?' Adelina held it out at arm's length. 'Fix it to the wall.'

A 6.15 a.m. start with tasks allotted every hour until 9.30 at night? More than fifteen hours of work! How would she go to school? The question was taking shape in Roza's head when her good intentions skidded back to her.

Be grateful, Roza.

She opened her mouth, hoping the words would come out right this time. 'I . . . I am happy to help, of course . . . Madam. I am used to helping my Mami with my little brother and cooking for our family. I even take turns cleaning the outside latrine.'

Roza paused. The woman's face was impassive.

Go on.

'I want to show my gratitude to you and your husband. So does my father. Um . . . his letter. I . . . I could not find it.'

'This?'

Straight away Roza recognised the blue-lined sheet of paper filled with Babi's untidy scrawl. She watched with horror as Adelina tore it down the middle. And then again. Scraps of paper drifted to the floor like snowflakes.

Adelina crossed her arms. 'I didn't read any apology for his contempt for family loyalty, his cowardice! What did he tell you, eh?' Her lips twitched. 'That you would attend a school for young ladies? Enjoy a better life here – new clothes, a room of your own?'

'My father said . . .'

'*My father said.*' Adelina's mincing mime rose to a roar. 'Listen to me, you scraggy little bitch. From now on, *I* decide what you do and where you go. Cross me and you will find out there are worse things than being a servant in this house.'

'A *servant*? But Aunty Sade . . .'

'My mother knew what was best for her brother, with his sickly wife and a daughter full of big ideas draining him dry. You think you're something special, don't you, *budalla*! That's what I shall call you. *Stupid girl!*'

'No! My name is Roza Noli!'

'Sending you over here . . . It's one less mouth for him to feed, isn't it?'

'That's not true! My father loves me. He wants the best for me.'

'Is that so?'

Roza flinched as Adelina stepped up close. 'So why do you think he sold you to us?'

Chapter Seven

SATURDAY WAS A TEST from the start. The washing was tinged pink when the cycle finished, earning her a slap. A lump like a piece of gristle stuck in Roza's throat. She swallowed it back. Crying wouldn't help.

Then Skender demanded scrambled eggs for breakfast. When she put them in front of him five minutes later, he pushed them away. He clutched his throat and pretended to gag. 'Did you puke on my plate, *budalla*?' he sneered.

Already he was taking his cue from his mother. And Uncle Jozif – his eyes glued as usual to the newspaper – was deaf to it all.

Later, Roza was drilled in the use of the kitchen and electrical appliances. It took her most of the afternoon to make a chicken stew. After the family had eaten, Roza put aside the small amount left to eat in her cell later.

The kitchen was empty apart from Jozif who was on his hands and knees searching under the sink for the shoe polish. She elbowed the kitchen door shut and drew in a deep breath.

'Sir, there has been a terrible mistake.' Keeping her voice down and with one eye on the door she added, 'Aunty Sade promised me I would attend an excellent school. I am clever, the top of my class, and my English is the best in the whole school. But your wife says—'

'Stop!' Jozif straightened up. He turned to face her, raising his hand like a traffic policeman. 'It is no good complaining to me. Now my wife is here, you must do as she tells you.'

'But Uncle, we are family. I have done nothing wrong. Why is she treating me like this?'

He placed his hand on the door handle and then stopped and turned to Roza. 'It's not because of anything *you* have done,' he said.

Monday 8.15 a.m. Stand by the front door with Albi wearing his coat, hat and gloves.

The little boy skipped around Roza's feet. He was making a game of pulling his hat and gloves off, throwing them as far up the stairs as he could. Adelina was in the middle of another angry outburst. Skender could not find his new shoes and was making his mother late. Roza stood by the front door not daring to move.

Adelina's heels click-clacked across the hall. 'What are your duties when you get back here? Have you memorised them yet?'

Skender came downstairs wearing his shoes and they left the house, Roza pushing the buggy. The cardigan Mami had knitted her was nowhere near thick enough for a day like this and the wind bit into her arms.

At the end of the drive, Mrs Pam's helmet hair appeared over the trunk of her car.

Roza winced. *No, no, please don't.*

'Welcome to Ridley Rd,' she gushed. She stuck her hand out. 'Pam Hardiman. I expect your daughter told you . . .'

Adelina sailed past without breaking her stride. 'We are very busy people, Mrs Hardiman. Don't bother calling again.'

Roza didn't dare look up but she heard Mrs Pam's sharp intake of breath. She hurried to catch up with Adelina.

'Well, have you?'

'Madam?'

'Memorised your list of duties, you stupid girl.'

'I am trying,' Roza said in a flat voice.

They had arrived at a footbridge at the far end of Ridley Road. The water was flowing fast, still swollen by the heavy rain. Albi strained against the straps, kicking his little feet up and down. Like Ylli, he wanted to get out and throw a stick into the water.

His mother crossed over and stopped in front of a glass-fronted church. A thick gold cross was suspended on the brickwork above. She rapped her fingers on the notice board. 'Midweek activities, Skender. *They* will keep you out of trouble.'

The boy pulled out an ear bud and stared sullenly at his mother.

Roza thought of their own little church back home with its lively Sunday services. Father Daniel had spoken to her the Sunday before she left.

'God is looking after you, Roza,' he said, touching her shoulder lightly on the way out.

She wanted to believe it. Even now, she prayed. Just because bad things happened it didn't mean God had abandoned you. She just had to get through each day and hope and pray that Adelina's heart would soften.

Up ahead, a bank of trees swayed in the wind. Roza glanced at the signpost – *Thorn Hill* – and the image of children playing. If she was going to be looking after the little boy every afternoon, they could go up to the playground sometimes.

Adelina wagged her finger as though she could read Roza's mind. 'You go straight back to the house after taking Albi to nursery and you remain there. If anyone asks why you are not at school you tell them you are sixteen and helping out with your younger brother because you haven't yet decided what to do with your future. And keep away from that interfering cow next door.'

No school and no going anywhere except Albi's nursery. It was all she could think of. How would she practise her English?

After another two or was it three more turnings – Roza hoped she wouldn't have to find her way back here – the sign for Skender's school appeared. *Greywalls Academy.*

A bell rang from somewhere in the school yard. Boys in black blazers scattered in different directions. Adelina straightened Skender's tie. His face reddened as boys queuing at the entrance elbowed one another and sniggered. Roza hung back. She wasn't going to feel sorry for him. At least he was *going* to school.

Adelina reappeared at the gate. 'Our home address and the directions to

Albi's nursery.'

Roza ran her eyes over the rough map Madam had drawn.

'You collect my son at what time?' Adelina was looking past her at the bus stop up the road.

'Twelve o'clock,' Roza said in a mechanical voice.

'See to it that everything is ready for supper at six sharp.' Adelina rested her hand briefly on Albi's head. Then she was gone, those dreaded heels click-clacking away from Roza for once.

She sagged against the railings. It felt like the stillness that settled after a storm. The little boy wriggled in his seat and rubbed his floppy kangaroo against his cheek. Roza crouched down and found herself smiling at him. 'Shall we find *your* school, Albi?'

It was less than five minutes away. Two large houses joined together in a side street. Children ran around inside a fenced-off area. As Roza lifted Albi out of his buggy one small boy flung himself against the wire and stared at them. Albi wrapped his arms tightly around Roza's neck, his sudden dependence on her pulling at her insides. It reminded her of how much she was missing Ylli.

Inside a willowy woman wearing large round glasses on a chain around her neck took charge, unbuttoning Albi's coat and hanging it on a wooden peg. 'We'll need your details for our records. Dr Braka didn't mention a nanny when he came to register.'

'I am his older sister. I have just finished school.' Roza completed the mantra just as Adelina had told her to.

The woman gave her a form to fill in and for the first time she had to sign her new name.

My name is Roza Noli! she wanted to shout.

Section break

Number 44 Ridley Road was silent and cold when she turned the key and instead of being thankful to be on her own at last, all Roza could think of was her class at home and what *they* would be doing this Monday morning. Stefanie alone now at the desk they'd shared, Mrs Cicu reading the next chapter of *Chronicle in Stone* to the whole class.

Another thought snagged on the edges of her memory. That piece of card Mrs Cicu had given her with the name and address of a man. She'd said Roza could contact him if she needed any help. But Roza had thrown it away. She scrunched her fists and slammed them against the landing wall. *Stupid, stupid!*

But the man's name – that would come back to her. *Must* come back to her. It was only last Tuesday. Less than a week ago, for heaven's sake. *Think, Roza, think!*

In the hall, the clock chimed ten. Already she was behind with her chores.

9.30 a.m. Make the beds; tidy and hoover the bedrooms.

Skender's room was still a mess. He'd left yesterday's clothes scattered across the carpet. And there was an empty crisp packet and a banana skin on the duvet. Roza nudged the hoover under his bed and picked up the small packet which emerged the other side.

Cigarettes! A pack of twenty . . . and already five missing.

She didn't need to read the warning on the side to know that smoking killed – her grandmother was dying of lung cancer.

Roza moved into Albi's room and sank on to the bed. According to Adelina's list she was to spend the time after lunch *entertaining* the little boy. *Entertain him?* Babi would have laughed out loud. It made Roza think of jugglers or a circus clown. At home she'd taken Ylli to the lake and let him paddle or skim stones. When it was too wet to be outside, she'd made up stories.

But Babi would not be laughing now, not if he could see what she had come to.

It was starting to rain. Roza raised her eyes to the darkening clouds and let her mind drift back to the day when everything changed.

Chapter Eight

One month earlier

'It will take us forty minutes to drive to Aunty Sade's, Babi. Can't we go another time?' Roza paused in the middle of scrubbing her hands. She was supposed to be at school after her morning chores, putting the finishing touches to her essay. If she *had* to leave at the end of term, she wanted it to be as the girl who had just bagged the prize-giving trophy.

Babi was not listening. 'Wear your white dress, Roza. In honour of the occasion.'

Mami, a seamstress before she'd married, had attached a new lace panel to the hem. When she'd seen it the night before, Roza had assumed it was a special order.

'It is the best cotton,' Mami whispered.

Roza took in the detail. The softness, the well-placed darts to show off her growing curves, the tiny, neat stitches. 'Thank you, Mami,' she said.

Her mother reached up and stroked her cheek. 'Wear it well, my daughter.'

Now, her parents' quarrelling voices pursued her as she slipped into the house to put it on. Mami shouting at Babi, Babi shushing her – trying to keep the peace. It was about money. It always was. He had his job at the garage, but even with the extras from Aunty, there was never enough to go around.

Roza clamped her hands over her ears and tried to think of prize-giving. She imagined herself winning an award. She was stepping up to the podium to thunderous applause when Babi's voice screamed out. 'You are not hearing me, Silvana. Sade has cut me off. She will not give me another lek!'

'Oh, you have not grown much.' Aunty had been a beauty in her youth. Her portrait, showing a straight-backed young woman with prominent cheek bones and flawless skin, hung in the hallway. Now, disappointment in her niece added to the sinking jowls. Roza fixed her own gaze on her feet, encased in the same scruffy black shoes she wore everywhere. Lately they had been pinching, but Aunty would not be interested in that.

'She is wearing her best dress to visit her favourite aunty.' Babi reached across and patted Roza's hand. She snatched it away. She hated the syrupy voice he used with his sister. Even more, she hated the way he talked about *her* as if she were still in fourth grade.

The maid appeared with a tray of tea and tiny cakes. Roza tried hard not to wrinkle her nose at the smell of body odour.

Aunty replaced her staff regularly. This girl with her skinny frame was different from the one who had scowled at her last visit.

'I have called you here for a very singular reason, Roza.' Aunty's eyes fluttered as she gave the 'r's in her speech their customary roll. 'A great opportunity awaits you, to move to England, to be educated there.'

The cake caught in Roza's throat and she coughed, spraying crumbs across the carpet.

Aunty paused and dipped her head. 'To continue. My daughter Adelina and her doctor husband, they are very successful with a good income and a fine home. They wish to share their good fortune with a family member who will most benefit.'

Roza scanned her memory bank. She had a vague recollection of meeting them at Aunty Sade's when it was just her and Lorik. But their faces were indistinct – a thin moustache on him, bullet-hole eyes for her, a whingeing boy tugging at his mother's skirt. And no one smiling.

'You have been specially chosen,' Aunty continued. 'You will live with them and in return for a few chores – light housework, helping with the little ones – they will provide for you.'

'Babi?' Roza could not look at him fast enough.

His fist dug into the small of her back. 'What do you say to that, my daughter?'

'Are you and Mami coming too?'

Roza gazed out of the window as Babi's car merged with the traffic on the autostrada. Concrete bunkers still littered the landscape from the Cold War and even with the windows closed there was a stink from the overflowing dumpsters. Plenty of people would be happy to be leaving such a place. But moving to England? It was hundreds of miles away and these relatives were strangers to her.

Did she have a choice? Neither Babi nor Aunty had asked if she *wanted* to go. Last week Babi had told her she had to leave school to look after Ylli. Had he asked Aunty for help or was the timing a coincidence?

'Who will help Mami now with Ylli?' Roza asked. That would be hard to bear – not watching her little brother grow up.

Babi took a long time answering. 'We will find a way. Your education is important.'

'I have never heard of this happening, Babi. Not to anyone I know.'

'These people are your cousins, Roza. And very wealthy. Families . . . they help each other out, share their good fortune. Is that so hard for you to understand?'

'Is she nice, my cousin?'

'Adelina? Yes, I think so.'

'But you do not know?'

'We have had no contact for more than ten years.' He huffed. 'I thought you would be grateful.'

'Oh, I am grateful, Babi. Truly.'

'This way you will be able stay at school. And not just *any* school. You are a clever girl, Roza. Your aunty knows that. In England you will have the education you deserve. And when you have passed all your examinations, who knows, you may be able to attend one of the great British universities.'

'Really?' Roza's mouth dropped open. She had not dared to imagine. Compared to such a glittering future, prize-giving at the village high school would be like winning a toy monkey at the travelling funfair.

Babi fell quiet. 'I want you to have the opportunities I never had, *drite e syrit*.'

Light of my eyes. He only ever used that phrase with *her*.

Roza did the maths in her head. 'Four years of school, that is a long time. Do you think my cousins will bring me with them when they come to visit? Or perhaps you and Mami could travel to England with Aunty Sade?'

'My sister never leaves the country. She has a fear of flying.' Her father lifted his hands. If he was about to say anything more, he thought better of it. He tightened his knuckles around the steering wheel. 'Let's go home. There is much to do. Four weeks will pass in a flash.'

***

Why do you think he sold you to us?
Had Babi really been that desperate? There was only one way to find out.

Chapter Nine

TWO WEEKS WENT BY. Every time Roza passed the phone she thought about picking it up. But if she rang Babi too soon, he would almost certainly tell her she had not given herself time to settle in. And Adelina could not keep up this hostile behaviour for ever. Snarling *budalla* at her, finding fault with almost everything she did.

Yesterday it had been the way Roza hoovered the carpet – she'd left the pile ruffled the wrong way. The night before, she had splashed sauce over the hob while serving up. Adelina had come up behind her with a bamboo stick and swiped her hard on the backs of her legs. It was Albi's birthday and Jozif and the boys were playing in the next room. Roza had to cover her mouth to stop herself crying out.

Today Albi fell asleep in his buggy on the way home from nursery. Roza lay him down on the couch in the lounge and went to pick up a plastic envelope lying on the doormat. A children's charity asking for donations – clothes, books, bric-a-brac, whatever that was. And stamped with large red letters – **MONDAY**. Roza left it on the windowsill where Adelina would see it. Not that she could imagine Madam giving anything away for free.

The light on the hall phone was winking. Someone had rung and left a message. Roza's heart skipped a beat. It might have been Babi, calling to find out how she was.

At home, it would be half-past one – the time he always spent in the office chasing up unpaid bills. Mr Miloti was a kind employer but working as a garage-hand had never suited Babi. Her father had wanted an education too. He would never have sent her to Britain for *this*!

It was hard to know what to think. If Aunty Sade *had* called time on helping her brother out, sending Roza to live with her daughter might have appeared the obvious solution. But had she made promises to Babi she knew to be false? *Light housework, helping with the little ones.* Hardly! Roza examined the peeling skin on her hands, her chipped fingernails. And as for the promise of a good school . . .

In the front room, Albi was stirring. Roza pulled out two slices of bread to make him a ham sandwich. She pulled out a third slice for herself, chewing it down in one go in case the little boy saw and told his mother.

'Mami come home now?'

Roza took his kangaroo from him and propped it up against the salt cellar.

'Come and eat your lunch, Albi. Roo can watch you.'

'Me want see Ben,' he whimpered.

Roza sighed. He had been asking for his old nursery friend all week.

'You can watch Thomas the Tank Engine later,' she said in a bright voice.

Albi stamped his foot. With a defiant look, he tipped his plate on to the floor and plodded up to his bedroom. Roza listened at the foot of the stairs. A few moments later *vroom-vroom* noises sounded through the ceiling. She stared at the phone. Albi wouldn't be down anytime soon.

What are you waiting for?

Praying she was remembering the numbers correctly, Roza hit the keys one by one and waited for the call to connect.

Her father's *Alo* (his voice always rising uncertainly at the end of the word, as though he had never used a phone before), brought a lump the size of a pebble to her throat.

'Babi!'

'Roza? Why are you calling?'

She breathed out sharply. 'It is a mistake, Babi. A dreadful mistake! My cousin is so unkind. She hits me and doesn't feed me properly and there is to be no school for me. You should hear the way she talks to me, Babi – the language she uses. Saying bad things about you too. I don't understand it.'

'Bad things about me?'

'Yes, and she calls me *budalla*, all the time. I hate it here!'

Raising her voice was the last thing she meant to do but the line was crackling and she did not want him to misunderstand. She waited for him to say something to fill the silence.

There was a rustle of papers. 'You are homesick, my girl. And I will write to you, I promise. But you must give yourself time to settle in with your cousins. The way they live now may be different to ours.'

Roza dragged her sleeve across her wet cheeks. Crying was not part of her plan either. 'I want to come home, Babi. I want to be with you and Mami and Ylli . . .'

'No!' The sudden change in his tone was like a punch to the stomach. 'That cannot happen.' The tremor in his breath was unmistakable. 'My dearest girl, I am so sorry, this is not what I hoped for. You must try harder to please your cousin. I will speak to your Aunty. Perhaps there has been some misunderstanding about the arrangement.'

'Mrs Cicu, Babi. Go and see her. She will know what to do. She gave me the name of someone to call but I—'

'Your teacher? This is nothing to do with her and she has, er . . . moved away. Now, you stay strong, Roza. Everything will be all right. But you must understand.' There was no mistaking the crack in his voice. 'There is *no* coming back.'

'Moved away. Are you sure, Babi? Mrs Cicu did not say anything . . .'

At Babi's end, a car engine was revving. And a voice Roza recognised. She pictured Mr Miloti mopping his forehead with the crisp white handkerchief Stefanie's mother gave him every morning.

Mr Miloti's voice persisted. But she could not let her father hang up. Not yet.

Babi? My cousin says you sold me.

She opened her mouth but the words caught in her throat.

'Roza, I must go. The line is bad and there is a customer waiting.'

An empty space opened up inside her. The little speech Babi parroted whenever he needed to get rid of a difficult customer.

The line clicked. He was gone.

Chapter Ten

It was all but hidden by brambles, the sign at the top of the lane next to Albi's nursery.

Marwood 1 mile.

She could go exploring! The day itself demanded it – the sky a brilliant blue, the air so cold her breath was coming out in cloudy puffs. But ignoring Adelina's demands could have bigger consequences. Roza was supposed to go straight back to Ridley Road.

She tied Albi's scarf around her neck. *She would do it!*

Monday the first of April. She was fifteen today.

Birthdays at home had never been anything special, though her twelfth had been good. All down to the bonus Mr Miloti had awarded Babi for selling three cars in one month. Mami had cooked Roza's favourite meal that night – *tave cosi*. Baked lamb with rice and yogurt. Her mouth watered just thinking about it. There was homemade baklava to follow and the whole family had sat around the fire, eating together. This year there were no birthday cards from home, and she was still waiting for a letter from Stefanie who had promised to write every week. Did any of them *have* her new address? Something else she didn't want to think about.

Roza dodged a muddy puddle. She reached the end of the lane and a wide expanse of green opened up. She stretched her arms. It was weird, being somewhere different from Thornley and after so much time in the house. A gull wheeled overhead, screeching and swooping low. A sudden gust of wind blew Roza sideways. She laughed out loud, twirling around and breaking into a run, feeling more alive than she had for weeks.

She stopped in front of a swing gate. A man in a puffer jacket pulled his barking dog aside to let her pass over the railway line.

She sprinted across the grass and dropped on to the stump of a tree. The wind was making her eyes water and her cheeks burn. She blinked at the big blue signboard beyond the perimeter fence.

BISHOP JOHN HIGH SCHOOL.

Was this the school Mrs Pam had talked about?

As though some unseen finger was beckoning, Roza crossed the road to the main gate. Now she could see it properly – a modern two-storey building behind mown patches of grass and neat flower beds.

At her school in Albania, the floors were bare concrete and the walls cracked and in need of a coat of paint. Sometimes there were not enough desks to go around. But however bad things were at home, she always felt safe there.

A bell rang. Children poured out of doors, swinging bags and peeling off noisily in different directions. A sudden urge gripped Roza to march up the drive and ask to see the principal, to explain what had happened to her; that she was fifteen years old and should be there too.

A car crawled down the drive and stopped next to her, signalling to turn out. A knot of girls followed behind, their voices high-pitched and giggly. Roza took in the details of the uniform – dark red blazers, swinging pleated skirts, a striped tie.

The shortest of the three, her eyelashes black with mascara, smirked at Roza. 'You lookin' at me or what?'

'Tash!' Her friends bumped one another and tittered.

She planted herself in front of Roza. 'Well, who *does* she think she is?'

Roza fixed her gaze firmly on her horrible ill-fitting shoes. Her face was on fire. Who *did* she think she was? Not someone who belonged in *this* school.

She turned away so they couldn't see her face burning. This had been a bad idea. She should get straight back to Ridley Road. The trouble was, when she finally got going, one road looked just like another and before she knew it she was meandering down a pavement filled with market stalls. Fresh meat and eggs at one, polished silver spoons and patterned china at the next. A woman passed her in a motorised trolley, pop music blaring from the radio hanging around her neck. Someone stopped Roza, asking for directions. It was all a bit much.

She crossed the road. There were fewer people on the other side.

'You look a bit chilly, lovey. Hoping to come inside, were you?'

She didn't see the woman until she was right up next to her. She stood there in a long apron and thick clogs. She was shorter than Roza with frizzy ginger hair pulled back in a blue hairband.

Roza tipped her head back to look at the sign creaking overhead. *Rainbow Cafe.* Through the window she could see a man in white overalls rolling paint up and down the far wall.

The woman leaned her shoulder into the door. 'We're running a bit late with the refurb. But we'll be open again next week with our new menu. Coffees, cakes, paninis. Books and CDs too. Come back then, why don't you?'

Roza shot a glance at the brown paper bag in the woman's hand. So that was where the wonderful smell was coming from. It made her feel hungrier than ever. She hadn't eaten since the evening before and then it was only the crusts from Albi's toast and an overripe banana destined for the bin. It would have been nice to go inside on her birthday. But, open or closed, it made no difference. She had no money. The only thing in her pocket was the house key to Ridley Road.

Books and CDs.

She started walking away. When she turned, the woman was still there looking at her.

'Is there a lending library in this village?' Roza asked.

'It's around the corner, lovey. You can't miss it. Just follow the bend in the road.'

The library wasn't what Roza was expecting. One of the windows was splintered like a spider's web and someone had daubed a rude word in white paint underneath it. But when she headed up the short path the door opened automatically, like she was a VIP. Inside it was all light and warmth and bright colours. And so many books – more than she had seen in her whole life, packed tightly upright on the shelves. She had goosebumps running up and down her arms.

Roza glanced around. No stern notices either like the lending library at home. *Talking prohibited. No food allowed.* And with so few books that they lay at odd angles or on their sides.

She settled at an empty table by the back window. Someone had left a newspaper. She should try to keep up with the news from home. But there was nothing about Albania. Her thoughts floated back to her phone call with Babi. Had he spoken to Aunty Sade yet? And how was Mami?

Mami. She had been so taken up with her own misery she hadn't thought to ask about her mother. Or had she been afraid to? Their last proper conversation hadn't ended well.

The heavy rains had lasted well into the new year. That morning they were rattling the corrugated roof of the outhouse. Roza woke to the stickiness of blood between her legs and crept into her parents' room to fetch one of the pads Mami kept in a box under the bed.

When she had cleaned herself up, she tapped her mother's shoulder. 'I will fetch you something to eat, Mami, before I sort out Ylli.'

Breakfast and one of the pick-you-up tablets the doctor had recommended. Her mother rolled over and stretched her arms above her head. She pushed

back the thick woven blanket and looked over Roza's shoulder at the rain-spattered window.

Talk to me, Mami. Tell me you will miss me.

Time was running out. In three days Roza would be gone.

'Your father has made the arrangements.' Mami's voice was flat. 'You are happy to be going.'

Roza wasn't sure if it was a statement or a question. 'I suppose so.' She shrugged and sat down on the edge of the bed. 'But I *will* miss you, Mami.'

Tears leaked out of her mother's eyes and she made no effort to wipe them away.

'Babi says my cousins are very wealthy people. Perhaps you and Babi can come to visit.' Second time around, the words had a hollow ring to them.

Her mother covered Roza's hands. Above them, Ylli was calling out.

'Never forget who you are, Roza Noli!' Mami said.

Now it was Roza's turn to look away. Mami was searching her eyes with an intensity she couldn't bear. 'Of course not!' *Why would she even say that?*

A deep sound rose up, like a sob. And Roza could not be sure whether it was Ylli above or her mother.

Mami never wanted her to have an education, she told herself fiercely as she scrubbed the latrine later. If she stayed in the village, she would end up just like her. Married young, and old before her time.

'Can I help at all?'

Roza looked up from the UK atlas she had taken off the bookshelf. She'd noticed the assistant with the straggly beard on the way in. A name badge hung around his neck. *Joe.*

'Your first visit?'

He had a nice lopsided smile. 'The lady at the cafe gave me directions,'

Roza replied.

'Ah, Wendy. So thoughtless of her to do the place up. Where does she think I'm supposed to eat?' He winked.

'Oh!' He was joking. Roza smiled back. Two friendly people in one morning. 'Can you tell me where Thornley Combe is exactly please? And how far from London? I have only just come to live here, you see.'

His eyebrows shot up. 'Your English is very good. Sorry, am I allowed to say that?'

Roza blushed. It was the first time she had received a compliment since she'd arrived.

He pulled a pencil from behind his ear and drew something in the empty space at the bottom of the paper. 'Okay, well let's see. If this is Oxford, then London is about 55 miles away. And Thornley Combe, that's about another four miles on from Oxford.'

Roza studied the wonky little triangle. 'Thank you.' She wasn't even sure why she had asked. Perhaps it was the thought of the man Mrs Cicu had said would help her. The journalist who lived in London.

'You're not at school then?'

Roza parroted her little speech. It sounded less convincing every time.

'Wendy's always on the lookout for an extra pair of hands.'

'You mean a job at the cafe? Oh no. I couldn't do that.'

It was a relief when a woman behind the desk called Mr Joe's name and waved the phone at him.

Roza turned her attention back to the main reason she had come in. Books. As she combed the shelves, piling one book on top of another, a crazy idea bubbled up. She might not be able to attend the *Bishop* or work in a cafe but she could come here some mornings while Albi was at nursery, couldn't she? She was a fast worker. As long as she kept up with her chores, Adelina need never find out.

Roza pushed the books she had chosen towards Mr Joe.

'Sorry, but you'll need to fill this form in before you can take any home.' He tilted his head. He could see she was disappointed. 'And don't forget to bring some ID with you.'

As Roza retraced her steps to Thornley Combe all she could think about was finding her passport. She hadn't seen it since handing it over to Jozif. If it was locked away somewhere in Adelina and Jozif's bedroom, as she suspected, she didn't know how she'd get hold of it.

Mrs Pam's car reversed down her drive knocking over a bulky plastic sack that had blown into the road. A chunky sweater was poking out where the bag had spilt. One of the charity bags. Whoever filled it had the right day, but a week late.

Roza hurried inside with it. The cream sweater on the top of the pile reached down to her knees but would do nicely to keep her warm at night. She dug deeper, discarding children's jeans and pink canvas shoes far too wide for her narrow feet.

Her breath caught. At the bottom, neatly folded, was a dark green duffel coat with cone-shaped buttons and sturdy loops as fasteners. Roza unfolded it and shook out the creases. She slipped her arms into the sleeves and gave a little twirl in the mirror. The cuffs were worn and one of the buttons was missing, but the lining was soft and fleecy. Imagine how snug and warm she'd feel taking Albi to nursery.

'Happy Birthday, Roza' she said to herself.

Tuesday 2nd April. 10.33 pm: phone call

Arben Noli Sade, at last! I have been trying to speak to you all week. I keep getting your answerphone message.

Sade I have been in Tirana on business. What is so urgent, Arben?

Arben Roza. (Pause) She rang me.

Sade I hope she asked permission first. Long-distance calls cost ...

Arben Sade, she was most upset. Adelina has told her she will not be sending her to school.

Sade No, I am sure that is not right.

Arben She also said that Adelina ... has struck her. More than once.

Sade Anything else?

Arben That she is spending all her time cooking, cleaning and caring for the small child. And that Adelina is bad-mouthing me.

Sade You are sure about all this?

Arben Roza would not make that up. And it is not so hard to believe. Forgive me, but she has been prone to violent outbursts in the past.

Sade She is over that now. It was a long time ago.

Arben Sade, this is not what we agreed for Roza. And it is what I feared – that Adelina has still not forgiven me. It's why I held back from agreeing to send her. But you persuaded me.

Sade Yes, it is ... disappointing.

Arben It is more than disappointing, Sade. This is my dearest daughter.

Sade And yet you *were* willing to let her go, Arben. And you have been paid handsomely. The money has helped you clear your debts, and now you can get medical help for your wife's problems? She must be grateful for that.

Arben Yes, but ...

Sade I will speak to Adelina. She gave me her word she would go easy on the girl. I will do what I can. I am still her mother. Good night, Arben.

Chapter Eleven

At the end of the week, Albi fell sick. Vomiting over the floor in the middle of the night.

As soon as Jozif woke her, Roza set about scrubbing the carpet.

'We have an early start tomorrow,' he said. He wiped the little boy's face with a flannel. 'We are going to view a possible boarding school for Skender. In Hertfordshire.'

This was news to her. Adelina grumbled about Greywalls School the way she did about most things: the amount of homework (*not enough*), the boys in his class (*a bad influence*). Even the head teacher was *too weak*. And Jozif had found the cigarettes – there had been a huge fuss about that. Skender's pocket money had been stopped. There had been threats to confiscate his Xbox. But no talk – in Roza's hearing anyway – of sending him away to school.

Jozif finished changing Albi into clean pyjamas.

Roza lifted him from his father's arms. 'He had better sleep downstairs with me if you are leaving early,'

Next morning, a note on the kitchen table in Jozif's handwriting told her they would be gone until Sunday evening. Roza breathed out a sigh. *Two whole days!*

By the time Albi was awake, she had run the soiled bedding through the washing machine. To her relief, the slice of toast and cup of water she encouraged him to eat both stayed down. The little boy pulled himself roughly on to her lap as they cuddled up on the sofa to watch CBeebies. Roza flinched and hissed. Her arm was still sore from the thumping Adelina had given her the night before. She'd locked her outside too, all because, according to Adelina, she'd made a poor job of cleaning Skender's rugby boots

Babi had promised to speak to Aunty Sade but already two weeks had passed and nothing had changed. Madam lashed out at her least misstep, railing against her family, telling her how spineless her father was, that *she* was useless just like him. It made no sense. Her father and Adelina hadn't seen one another for years. Perhaps she should ring Babi again. Roza bit her lip. Not after what he had said last time . . . *No coming back.*

'More food,' Albi jumped down from the sofa. He was definitely feeling better.

By lunchtime, the rain which had been falling all morning had stopped. Thin sunshine pressed through the clouds. It was bright enough to walk up to the playground at Thorn Hill.

Roza strapped Albi into his buggy. 'Our little secret,' she said, pressing a finger against her lips.

By the time they reached the top, he was asleep. Roza's armpits were damp. She undid the toggles on her new coat and let it flap open. The view was her idea of a perfect English landscape. She could see for miles. A cluster of houses tucked among spindly trees, sheep grazing on the hills, even a train. She watched it disappear into a tunnel, thinking about the passengers; where they had come from, where they might be heading. Were any of them facing nasty surprises at the end of their journey? Like she had.

Now she thought about it, the signs had been there from the day she left the village.

Babi had been waiting for her on the front step when Roza returned from buying bread and milk for breakfast. Aunty Sade was there too, in her fur coat and boots.

'The date has been brought forward, Roza.' Babi faltered. 'Your flight is today.'

It was a joke, surely. 'I can't, Babi. You know it's prize-giving. You and Mami are coming.'

Aunty hugged her coat tighter. 'Fetch your case now, Roza.'

'Where is Mami? And . . . and Ylli?' Breakfast time and there was no noise. What was going on?

Her father cleared his throat. Something else he didn't want to tell her then. *'Gjyshe* took a turn for the worse in the night. They are on the early bus. Lorik has gone to help with the baby.'

Aunty clapped her hands. 'Now, Roza! Go and change. We must leave. The flight for London takes off at six.'

In a fog, Roza went indoors to change into the hideous clothes Aunty had laid out for her.

When she stepped back outside, Babi's tight hug almost squeezed the breath out of her. She went to pull back, feeling the tremor in his body as he clung on.

'Go well, *drite e syrit*,' he mumbled in her ear.

He opened the car door and it was only when he turned to walk back to the house that Roza spotted it – the thick white envelope sticking out of Babi's back pocket. What was in it? Photos of her cousins and their children, details of where she was going, her new address in the UK? Or something else?

Albi squealed in his buggy and kicked his feet. Roza unbuckled his strap and watched him climb the steps of the slide, throwing himself down and waving to her at the bottom.

Tears ran down her cheeks. She knew now what had been inside that envelope. She stretched her arms wide, letting the breeze ruffle her hair.

She might be only fifteen but she knew how things worked. You could not simply take something back, could you? Not if you had sold it.

28th April: Email

**To: michaelm75
From: cicukam**

Hello Michael

I hope you and Juliana are OK and things are back to normal after the flooding.

I have a favour to ask. One of my girls – my best girl! – has gone missing in the UK. She is the one to whom I gave your address should she be in trouble. Roza Noli is her name. As I have heard nothing from you, I am assuming she has not contacted you. Her family arranged for her to fly to Heathrow at the end of February to move in with a cousin. Better education, better life – you know how it goes. It seems my worst fears have been realised. No one, not even the girl's best friend, has heard from her since then.

I called to see her family but their reluctance to talk to me (or even look me in the eye), has persuaded me that something has gone badly wrong for Roza. It's like looking for a needle in a haystack, I know, but is there anyone in the police you might contact to try and find her?

Gratefully,

Kamila.

Chapter Twelve

Roza eased the straightened-out paper clip from the keyhole for the fourth time and sighed with exasperation.

It was Lorik who had shown her how to pick a lock. After Mami had given birth to Sindi and the two of them had taken Ylli for a walk and forgotten their key.

You have to be patient, sis. First time is never easy.

Roza held her breath and, making sure the other paper clip was in place, *(the one that acted as a tension wrench – see Lorik, I remembered that!)* inserted the length of wire once more and gave it a little jerk to the left. *Fifth time lucky? Yes!* The lock gave way and she was able to rotate the handle. Why hadn't she thought to do this before?

The door swung open to a heavy stale smell. Roza wrinkled her nose. The bed was unmade, clothes spilled out of half-closed drawers and paper tissues littered the carpet. She hadn't been inside the Brakas' bedroom since the day Adelina arrived. That was three months ago.

Now, finally, she could look for her passport – get a library card and bring some books back to Ridley Road. It would make studying easier. Twice in the last month the books she'd wanted had been out on loan.

And she wanted her passport back. It was hers! And one day, with help, she would need it to travel back to Albania. She had long since given up praying for Adelina's heart to soften, but something would change. It had to. She wasn't staying imprisoned here for ever.

Roza made a quick search of the chest of drawers and the floor to ceiling wardrobe. The top shelf – her best bet, reachable only with the help of a folding step stool – yielded nothing. She scanned the rest of the room. Time was running out if she was going to make it to the library before collecting Albi. Where else could it be? Her eyes settled on Adelina's bedside cupboard.

Roza kneeled down in front of it and pulled hard. There was no lock but something was jamming the door. Multipacks of chocolate bars tumbled out on to the carpet. Her mouth filled with saliva as she picked one up. Without another thought, she tore into the wrapping and bit into it.

She closed her eyes. The sugary mix of milk chocolate and thick squidgy centre coated her tongue and the roof of her mouth. She held it there for a few more minutes before letting it slip slowly down her throat.

There was other stuff in the cupboard – she could see it now she'd opened her eyes. She blinked hard and sat up. *What was she doing?*

With her hands she scooped out the the cupboard's contents on to the floor. More empty wrappers than she could count, a nail file, half a dozen dog-eared novels and a packet of birthday cards in a cellophane packet. And, at the back, a white cardboard box.

Roza placed it on the carpet and lifted the lid. It was filled almost to the top with official-looking documents. Drivers' licences, Jozif's medical qualifications, the boys' birth certificates. Roza sifted through them one by one. Her passport had to be here.

She was halfway through when a cream-coloured booklet jumped out at her. *Family Allowance*. Her new name – Roza

Braka – typed in bold, above those of Skender and Albi. She stared at it. Adelina was receiving money for her from the UK government. Nearly one hundred pounds every month.

She had just finished going through the rest when the hall clock chimed. Half-past ten already. She breathed out sharply. *That was a waste of time!*

She picked up the box to return the papers. A folded envelope was wedged at the bottom and hadn't fallen out with the rest of the contents. When she prised it out the envelope was crisp and new, not like the others. Inside were two identical sheets. Copies of her birth certificate. Only it wasn't really hers – it had Jozif and Adelina named as her father and mother. Roza focussed on the column headed date of birth. It was the same as on her passport. A whole two years before she had been born.

There was someone different behind the library desk this morning. But this man didn't smile and the way his eyes travelled up and down her face reminded her of the man at passport control. She half-expected him to say he knew her birth certificate was a fake but finally he handed it back with her new library card.

She sat down at the only free table near the front desk with a textbook about the geography of Eastern Europe. When she found herself starting the same paragraph for the fourth time she pushed the book to one side and slumped back.

Why was she so shocked Aunty Sade was able to obtain a birth certificate for her? Her father used to boast that Aunty had *friends in high places.* She'd helped him get out of paying his taxes. But did Babi know his sister had used those connections to wipe out Roza Noli's existence. Was that what Mami had meant? *Never forget who you are, Roza.*

Peals of laughter rang through the library foyer. Roza looked up. The girl in dungarees who read to little kids at Story Time was now helping a boy hang pictures on the wall. Dark hair curled over the collar of his jacket. *Live Life and Surf* was splashed across the back. He straightened the frames and stepped back to check they were level. His lips moved but Roza couldn't hear what he was saying. It must have been something funny though because the girl was shaking like a paint mixer. People looked up to see what was going on. The man at the desk even put a finger on his lips to shush them.

The boy packed up his rucksack with the paintings they'd taken down. She could see him properly now. He was mixed race, his face scattered with freckles. He hooked his bag carefully on to his back and pulled a beanie over his head. With a casual wave he was out through the door.

Roza dragged a newspaper towards her and scanned the headlines.

Anything to take her mind off this morning's revelations.

A photo of a young girl whose soldier father had been killed in the war in Iraq filled a good part of the front page. Roza groaned inwardly. She flipped to the inside pages.

Trafficking ring uncovered as banker jailed for keeping Romanian girl as slave.

She held the paper closer. Phrases jumped off the page at her. *A distant relative. The promise of free education. Forced to work fourteen hours a day.*

The photo showed a man and a woman making every effort to hide from the camera lens. His hand was splayed across his face. She was using a scarf to cover her mouth and nose.

Picking up from the beginning, she read the report again, slowly. It wasn't just *this* girl's story. It sounded like hers too.

At the foot of the page, a box in small print described the newspaper's investigation into something called *Child Traffick-*

ing. Reporters from the UK had visited hotspots in Europe to find out what was going on; to establish who was responsible for what they called *this evil trade*.

Roza dug her fingers into her temples. *Child Trafficking*. She had heard that phrase before.

For families living on the edge of poverty in countries like Ukraine, Romania and Albania the temptation to sell a child as a way out of debt is increasing. But these trafficking networks are ruthless and growing in number, and the promise of a better life abroad is a hollow one.

Yes. Yes! Was this what had happened to her?
Sold to a member of her extended family.
Check.
Passport confiscated. No schooling. Beaten and abused.
Check. Check. Check.

A wave of panic pressed down on Roza's chest. It felt as though all the air had been sucked out of the room. Tugging on her coat and backpack she lurched towards the exit, vaguely aware of Mr Joe calling a cheery *hello* to her on his way in. She flattened her palms against the automatic doors as they slowly parted.

She started to run. *Rainbow Cafe* and all the other shops passed by in a blur. Around one corner, then another, and before she knew it she was hurtling along a road bordered by a cemetery with a line of black limousines parked along the kerbside and a row of shops she'd never seen before. Her legs and lungs were burning. It must be lunchtime. Albi would be waiting for her, his Thomas the Tank Engine bag on his back, but there was no space in her head to think about that now.

She swung into a lane and leaned heavily against the metal railings. The cold air was just what she needed. She gulped at it, pulling it into her lungs.

Trafficking. The word pierced her like a bullet, the memory firing something up in her brain.

Mrs Cicu! She had come to see Babi just a few days after their visit to Aunty Sade. Mami was there too but it was just *their* voices she could make out. Babi shouting, angry and defensive. Mrs Cicu calm and polite as always but not backing down either, using words that made no sense. *Risk. Danger.* What was that about? And *traffic*?

Roza had retreated to the backyard then, picked up Ylli's ball and tossed it back and forth against the wall. The words bounced around her head like ping-pong balls.

Now she understood. Mrs Cicu hadn't been talking about cars and buses or crossing the road safely.

Roza wrenched the newspaper out of her bag.

They wouldn't let me go out. I had no friends. My job was to clean and cook and look after their baby but they didn't pay me anything. It has been like that for the past five years.

Five years!

'I will not be that girl!' Roza screamed.

A bent old couple crossing the road gave her a sideways look and hurried on.

She slid down the railings and buried her head between her legs. She didn't know how, not yet, but she *would* get away. Back to Albania. Back to her family. If she didn't – five years, maybe more – would be her fate too.

A boy on a bike was cycling slowly towards her from the other end of the lane, his wheels clicking. Roza waited for him to pass.

Only he didn't.

'Hey, are you ... er ... OK?'

She peered up through laced fingers. It was the boy from the library.

'You don't look very good, if you don't mind me saying.' He was looking down at her, his legs planted either side of the front wheel.

'Thanks.' Roza sniffed.

'Hey, don't take this the wrong way. I mean, I'm not trying to pick you up or anything but you look like you could do with a coffee?'

He'd made it into a question, his voice going up at the end.

'My aunty's got this cafe not far from here.'

'No. I have to go.' Roza clambered to her feet. She zipped up her bag, turning her back so he couldn't see the mess her face was in.

'Where are you going?' The kindness in his voice nearly creased her.

She sucked in a deep breath. 'None of your business!'

She pulled up her hood. In the distance there was a rumbling noise of traffic. Perhaps she could hitch a ride to London. That was what the girl in the paper had done in the end, where she found someone to help her.

Five minutes later, Roza was staring down a road with two lanes of traffic thundering along in both directions. Traffic lights loomed ahead, road signs in thick black letters – **Oxford, London.** Below them in smaller print, an arrow pointing right.

Warridge Police Station.

Police forces across the world are working together to bring child trafficking networks to justice...

With sudden clarity, she knew what she had to do.

Her feet flew across to the strip of grass dividing the traffic. She felt the rush of air as a bus driver blasted his horn. A woman glared and lowered her window, her words carried away on the wind. In the distance, a siren was blaring. If she could just make it across....

She didn't see the HGV until it was bearing down on her.

Chapter Thirteen

Roza had no idea what had happened after she locked eyes with the driver of the lorry; how she was now sitting in the back of a police car parked in a lay-by.

'What were you doing on the dual carriageway?' The sergeant took off her hat with its chequered band and placed it in her lap. It had flattened her blonde hair like a pancake.

'Roza!'

When had she told the woman her name? She tried opening her mouth but no words would come.

'It's OK lass, nothing to be afraid of.' The man passed her a blanket and smiled. 'Think we should get her checked out at Olly's?'

The hospital on the far side of town. Jozif worked there sometimes.

'She's OK.' The sergeant didn't look up, just carried on writing in her little notebook.

'If that lorry driver hadn't braked just in time.' The policeman shook his head. 'Good thing we were coming through.'

A wave of nausea swept over Roza. It was coming back to her now; why she had been in such a hurry to get to the police station. She folded her hands across her backpack and sat up straight.

'My home is in Albania,' she said, forcing the words out in her best English and trying to keep the tremor out of her voice.

'My parents do not have much money, so they arranged for me to come to this country. To live with my wealthy cousins. But my life here...' She choked back a sob. 'It is worse, much worse. A better life, that is what I was promised. But these people – all they want is someone to work for them sixteen hours a day. I have to clean and cook *and* look after their little boy. Adelina, the woman, she beats me – and I don't get proper food to eat...'

She saw them trade glances before Sergeant Colley's face folded into a frown. 'That's quite a story, young lady.'

'Yes, but it is not a *made-up* story. I am telling you the truth. I am only fifteen; I should be at school.' Roza yanked the newspaper out of her bag and unfolded it. 'Look! What happened to this girl has happened to me too.'

The woman's eyes ran over the report. Perhaps now they would believe her. The British police were good people, not like at home where they expected a bribe to get things done.

They left her on her own and she could see them on the grass verge talking. But only for a minute.

The sergeant slid back into her seat. 'We are going to take you home now, Roza.' Her tone was firm and her hand shot up when Roza tried to interrupt. 'We'll talk to your parents – the people you say have done these things to you – and see what they have to say.'

Fear rolled over Roza in an icy wave. 'No, I beg you! You cannot do that! What has happened to me is called child trafficking. Have you not heard of it? The newspaper said police—'

'Come on now, what's your address?'

Roza laced her fingers together tightly. *And she thought she could trust the British police to do what was right.*

'We'll have to search your bag if you don't tell us where you live.'

The scrap of paper Adelina had given her was still in there. This woman would find it easily enough.

'44 Ridley Rd,' she said miserably.

They were there in less than ten minutes.

'Roza, where have you been?' Adelina arrived at the foot of the drive as soon as the policeman opened the car door. She pawed Roza's arm.

Roza recoiled. 'Don't touch me!' The falsetto voice, tears pooling in Adelina's eyes – they must see she was putting on an act.

Albi crept up behind Roza rubbing Roo against his cheek.

'Is your husband here now, Mrs Braka?' Sergeant Colley said when they were inside

'He will be down directly,' Adelina replied. She opened the door to the front room. 'Please, come in here.'

The policeman sat down and laid his peaked cap on the arm of the sofa. Roza edged as close to him as she dared, fixing her eyes on his big black shoes. As long as the police were here, she was safe.

Hearing Jozif's voice, she looked up. He was still in his work suit, his shirt collar hanging open. He didn't look happy to be called out of afternoon surgery.

Sergeant Colley stood up. 'Is this your daughter, Dr Braka?'
'Yes, that's right.'

The sergeant explained how they had found Roza and how reluctant she had been to come home.

Adelina bobbed her head like a nodding dog, as though none of this was a surprise to her. 'Oh, Roza. You have been telling tales again.' Her eyes were wide with reproach. 'I'm afraid our daughter has a vivid imagination, Sergeant. Has she also been telling you we are not her parents and that we have been ill-treating her?'

Roza leaped to her feet. She *would* make them listen to her! 'Everything I have told you is the truth. Can't you see they are acting? They are *not* my parents!'

Adelina turned away as though that was the last straw. She sniffed. 'Jozif, please fetch Roza's birth certificate.'

'No! Ask them to show you my room!' Roza shouted. 'It's a laundry room, with only a tiny window to see out of. I don't have a proper bed, just an old couch they were going to throw out.'

All the time she had been speaking, Jozif was dabbing at beads of sweat on his forehead. A light went on in Roza's head.

No! No!

Jumping up, she tore through the hall and flung her cell door open. No couch, no bag of clothes, just the machines. She jabbed her finger at the empty space. 'The couch was there. They've moved it!'

Behind her, Adelina's voice was quiet and controlled. 'Your room is upstairs, Roza. As soon as you have chosen the wallpaper, your father is going to decorate it. You know that.' She turned to the sergeant. 'What a monstrous idea to imagine we would put our child in here. Please, come and see.'

She's going to show them Albi's room.

The policeman nudged Roza towards the stairs and followed her up.

Anyone could see it looked like a room for a girl with the strawberry wallpaper. A pile of Albi's soft toys had even been arranged on the bed. The sergeant went straight to the wardrobe. The dresses and tops Roza had seen in the black bag were hanging on the rail now. The woman eased the bottom drawer open and picked out a lacy vest and a pair of white socks. She raised an eyebrow.

Roza's arms prickled with cold. *Adelina knew this might happen and she had prepared for it when Roza went missing.*

'Sadly, our daughter has always had behavioural problems,' Adelina continued as the party filed back downstairs. 'Fortunately, my husband is a General Practitioner. We are arranging for her to see a psychologist at his practice.'

The policeman examined the birth certificate Jozif had produced. 'This all looks to be in order.' He sounded sorry.

'It's a fake.' Roza put her finger on her birthdate. 'I was not born for another two years. I was fifteen in April.'

No one was taking any notice. They were by the front door. Sergeant Colley picked up her hat and spoke in a low voice to Jozif. Her colleague touched Roza's shoulder. 'Make sure you get the help you need, young lady.'

Roza went into the kitchen to pour herself a cup of water. She sat down at the kitchen table. Albi slipped in from the back room where the TV was still on. He climbed on to her lap. The front door closed with a firm thud.

Roza pulled Albi's warm body tight to her chest.

Click-clack. Adelina planted herself in front of Roza, her eyes blazing like little globes of fire. If she were a boxer in the ring raising gloved hands, it could not have been clearer. She had won and they both knew it.

'Adelina. . .' From the door, Jozif's voice sounded a note of warning.

'Take Albi out to the park . . . anywhere. *I* will deal with this little witch.'

Jozif beckoned silently to Albi and when he wouldn't move, prised him gently off Roza's lap.

As soon as the door was closed Adelina yanked Roza to her feet. She pinned her arms against the door frame and drawing her head back spat in her face.

Roza heaved. A glob of spittle was hanging from her lips. As she shook her head from side to side like a wet dog, Adelina jerked her knee upwards. A fireball of pain tore through Roza's stomach and she crumpled on to the floor rocking and retching, fighting for breath. The cupboard door clicked – it was the one where Skender kept his rugby boots. The *dirty cupboard* Adelina called it.

'Get up!' she snarled. She was brandishing a walking stick. It was thick and gnarled and Roza remembered Jozif telling her it had been passed down by his grandfather.

'You're supposed to stand on the mat when I speak to you.'

Roza forced the words out. 'I . . . can't . . .' She gripped the kitchen table leg and tried to lever herself upright.

'Can't what? Stand up? Walk? Didn't have any trouble walking this morning, did you?'

Thwack! The stick tore into Roza's skin. Blood streamed down her shin. More blows – this time to her thighs and back – sent her careering against the cooker.

Adelina straightened herself, panting hard. 'You worthless piece of trash. Try walking anywhere now after all the trouble you've made for us. If those two go poking around, they'll find out you weren't living with us in Brighton.'

Roza crumpled on to the cold tiles and curled into a ball. Any minute now, please God, she'd pass out. She waited for the next whack but it didn't come.

Adelina took a step back. She was panting, almost bent double. She stabbed the stick against Roza's backside.

'You can *crawl* to where you're spending the night. On your hands and knees, bitch! You're no better than a dog.'

The door to the dirty cupboard was open. A black hole, barely a few feet high. Roza shrank back, taut with terror.

'A night in there will make you think again about telling any more tales.'

31st May: Answerphone message from Sade

Listen to me carefully, Arben. You must stop pestering me. I have put a block on your number so do not try to ring me again with your incessant questions. And I have shut up the house and moved, so don't bother trying to find me. You have to let the matter drop. I cannot be held responsible for my daughter's actions towards Roza if she thinks you intend to renege on the agreement.

Chapter Fourteen

June

'You coming in for a hot drink, lovey?'

The woman finished rubbing at the fingerprints on the cafe window and narrowed her eyes. She was shorter than Roza remembered, with wide hips and a mouth that looked as though it was ready to break into a smile. Which it did now.

'I remember!' She smiled and wagged a finger. 'You were here when we were closed for the refurb.' She leaned her shoulder into the door and gave a dramatic shudder. 'Come on in. It might be June but it's bloomin' Baltic out here today.'

Almost all the tables were taken and the noise felt like an assault on Roza's ears. The coffee machine hissing behind the counter, the buzz of chatter. Apart from 44 Ridley Road and the near-silent library she hadn't been indoors anywhere for months.

The woman pulled out a seat in the far corner next to a wooden trug of children's toys. 'Sit down, lovey. Take the weight off.' She murmured something to a thickset woman behind the counter who helloed a cheery greeting.

Roza hooked her bag onto the back of the seat and winced. Some movements were still painful even though ten days had passed and the bruises faded to yellow.

She took in the colourful decorations. A hand-painted rainbow filled most of the wall facing her. Underneath it, animals filed two by two into Noah's Ark. She remembered Babi reading her the Bible story and tracing her fingers over the rainbow.

On the wall alongside her there were paintings – four canvases arranged in a diamond pattern. The colours – soft blues and pinks and oranges – ran into one another giving her a fluttery feeling in her chest.

When she turned back, the pleasant cafe lady put a plate down in front of her. A crusty roll with a slice of bacon poking out at either end.

Roza's mouth filled with saliva. 'This is for me? But I don't have . . .'

The woman patted Roza's hand. 'There's no charge, lovey, if that's what you're thinking. Yesterday's leftovers. You're doing me a favour. Only end up in the bin.'

Leftovers! Roza wanted to tell her what they looked like where *she* lived.

'I'm Wendy, by the way.' The woman held out her hand to shake Roza's. 'And this is my cafe.'

Roza did the same. It felt strange holding another person's hand. 'I am Roza Noli,' she said.

She filled her mouth with the soft bread and bacon. Mr Joe's words came back to her. *Wendy's always on the lookout for an extra pair of hands.* She hadn't been ready for a job then but she was now.

'Not at school then?' Wendy was looking at her properly now. 'You look a bright young thing, lovin' books and all. Joe said he'd seen you at the library.'

A sudden commotion at the door made them both look up. A woman who looked older than Mami with a crying toddler at her side was having trouble manoeuvring a double buggy inside.

'She'll have my new paintwork off.' Wendy hurried to the door.

Roza licked the tomato ketchup off her fingers. At least she was saved from having to recite Adelina's *Not sure what to do about my future* mantra. Was it really only an hour ago she had shimmied out through the tiny top window? It was surreal. She counted back. Ten days ago . . .

The click-clack of heels through the kitchen. Albi wailing for Roo. The pips on the radio. Roza had counted eight – it must be morning then. Her leg was throbbing and there was a dreadful stink – she must have wet herself. Her nose was tickling too but with one hand pinned to her side by the crate of shoes and the other too stiff to move she couldn't reach to scratch it. She pressed her lips together and held her breath. A sneeze would make things twice as bad.

The front door closed. Voices disappeared down the drive. Then all was quiet.

It would be hours before Adelina and the boys returned and there was no guarantee Roza would be released even then. She tried reciting Kadare's *Longing*, the poem they had been studying at school before she left. But she soon gave up. It was difficult to think of anything other than spiders and her own misery.

There was a loud noise from the hall. Hurried footsteps. Then a sucking sound as the cupboard door was jerked open.

'My God! She told me she'd locked you in your room.'

Roza shielded her eyes from the rush of light as Jozif dragged her out by her legs. He transferred his hands to her armpits and hoisted her on to a chair like a rag doll. She felt like one too. One wrong move and she'd be on the floor.

'Water,' she managed to gasp.

While she gulped down a second glass Jozif bathed and dressed the bloody wound on her shin and the split above her eyebrow where she'd fallen against the kitchen table. There were bruises – too many to count. Roza was determined Jozif would see them all – her back, her thighs. She even opened her blouse to reveal the marks blooming across her chest where she had fallen against the crate.

'Adelina is sorry she lost her temper,' he said when he had finished.

Oh, that's all right then, if she's sorry! She only beat me half to death.

'She has taken the boys to stay with my sister in Reading for half term.' He emptied the bowl of mucky water in the sink, explaining that in future he would be the one dropping Albi off at an all-day nursery. 'Adelina will pick him up after work,' he added.

So Roza wouldn't be going out any more? There was a fog inside her head but she could work that out all right.

'These tablets will help with the pain.' Jozif refilled the glass and helped Roza into her cell.

He disappeared for a few minutes, returning with the black bag full of the girls' clothes she had seen hanging in Albi's wardrobe. He left them at her feet as if they might make amends for what Adelina had done to her.

Later, easing them gently over the parts that were still too painful to touch, Roza pulled on a pair of baggy tracksuit bottoms and three jumpers, one on top of the other. They did the job of warming her up but she still couldn't stop her legs jerking as though they were plugged into an electric socket. She supposed it was the shock.

After that she slept for what felt like hours on the mattress Jozif had produced for her on her first night. The sofa must still be in the garage.

She didn't remember much until he woke her the next day.

'You need some fresh air,' he announced after she'd had something to eat. 'And exercise.'

Roza wasn't sure she could even stand without keeling over. But when she hobbled outside into the warm sunshine, the air smelled like clean linen and she was glad she'd made the effort. She dropped heavily on to a canvas chair Jozif had found in the garage. There were roses budding, and honeysuckle – the same sweet-scented bush Mami had planted on her vegetable patch.

Jozif was in her cell, his shadowy shape fiddling with the catch on the top window. Minutes later, lifted by the breeze, it flew open.

Over supper that evening, Jozif announced, 'It will be better if you remain here from now on.'

Roza looked up. They were sitting at the kitchen table picking through spaghetti and meatballs which were as hard as bullets.

'The house . . . the garden.' He waved a hand.

Roza speared a piece of meat. So that was why he had removed the lock on the window.

'You must try not to upset her again,' he said.

She must try not to upset *Adelina*? Roza let her spoon and fork clatter on to the plate.

Jozif's head shot up. 'What do you expect me to say? You know this is the arrangement your family agreed to.'

'Not to *this*! Being locked up like a prisoner!'

He topped up his glass of raki and drank it down to the bottom. His chin waggled from side to side.

'There is something you need to know,' he said finally. 'Adelina and your father – there is some bad blood between them.'

Wendy sat down again with a bump and fanned her face with a paper napkin. 'So, what do you do all day if you're not at school?'

Roza blinked herself back to the hubbub of the cafe. 'I tidy the house and prepare meals for our family,' she said carefully. She flattened her hands between her knees.

'I bet you've got a string of them GCSEs. You should be studying A levels or whatever it is they do these days.'

'Do you have any jobs?' Roza blurted out.

If Wendy was surprised, she didn't show it. 'I can always do with somebody to wash the dishes. It's only me and Carla. My nephew's supposed to be here by now. But he's let me down *again*. Second time this week.' Wendy tutted. 'I shouldn't complain really, he's trying to get a proper job.'

'You mean *today*?'

'Kitchen's a bit of a mess and I haven't got time to sort it out.' Pink spots bloomed on Wendy's cheeks. 'I'd pay you the going rate of course.'

Roza bit down on her bottom lip. *She'd be well hidden in the kitchen.* 'I'll have to leave by half-past two,' she heard herself saying.

She wiped around the washing up bowl. The clean dishes were stacked neatly in the wall cupboards, the surfaces shining. She had even found time to scrub away the grimy stains on the hob.

She looked through the hatch. The lunchtime rush had passed. The cafe was empty apart from Mr Joe tucking into a meat pie and salad, a book propped up against the pepper pot. He glanced up as though he knew she was looking at him. She gave him a small wave. He had done her a favour.

'Proper little worker bee, aren't you?' Wendy said, coming in and looking around approvingly.

Roza frowned. *Worker bee?*

'Think we deserve a bit of lunch ourselves now.' Wendy set two bowls of soup on the worktop.

She pushed one towards Roza. 'Carla's leek and potato. Tuck in, lovey!' Wendy blew on the soup before taking a mouthful. 'Jason's mum's in Catford, you see. She's been in a bit of a state since his grandad died so Jason's moved in with me while he gets himself sorted out. He's a good lad really. But he's like you, dropped out of school.' She pulled a face. 'Didn't do so well in his GCSEs last year.'

Roza swallowed quickly and coughed. 'Sorry . . . who?'

'Jason. My nephew. What he's going to do with his life, I just don't know.' Wendy clicked her tongue. 'He's doing some part-time course at the local college but it's not really his cup of tea. I keep telling him, *you're seventeen now lovey; you should have some idea*.' Her face brightened. 'You'll get to meet him if you come again. There's a job for you in the kitchen any time you want it.' She pulled an envelope out of her apron. 'You'd better get going. It's gone two.'

Outside, Roza eased the flap open. Twenty pounds! The first money she'd seen since her arrival in England.

She fastened the toggles on her coat. Across the road a group of boys were messing around, catcalling and yelling outside the 8-till-late. They were in uniform – the same black blazers and striped ties as Skender.

A lanky ginger-haired boy tossed a shoe high into the air. Another lad hopped towards it, followed by jeers, but before he could get there it was in the air again. Back and forth it flew. He didn't stand a chance. Roza felt sorry for him. His cheeks were growing redder by the minute.

The shoe ended up in the road. The smallest of the boys bounded off the pavement. Grinning boldly, he held it aloft then swung round to high-five the ginger-head. Roza thought her heart would stop. It was Skender.

Chapter Fifteen

Roza crept up the garden path. She half-expected to find Jozif had played a trick on her and tightened the catch on the window. Or worse, now that Adelina was back from staying with Jozif's sister, she would be waiting for her. But wriggling back inside proved no harder than shimmying out. Roza let out a breath as her feet touched the floor. She had got away with it. For now, anyway.

And the couch was back in her cell. Indeed, everything was as it was before Adelina had laid into her. Frustration rushed through her. So much for her hopes that first night that the kind policeman would return in time to see what Adelina had done to her. It wasn't going to happen.

She sank down on the cushions. First Babi. Then Aunty Sade. Now the British police. Adults she should have been able to count on. They had all let her down, telling untruths themselves or not seeing through the lies of others. If she was going to break free for good there was only one person she could count on and that was herself.

As she undressed that night, Roza thought about the regular hours at *Rainbow*. And all the reasons to turn them down. The risk of being found out to start with – what if Skender had seen her today? Plus, she didn't really know Wendy. On top of that there were the extra jobs Madam would add to her list to keep her occupied now she was no longer looking after Albi.

She pummelled the cushion that acted as a pillow and lay down, linking her hands behind her head. If she *didn't* take the job, how would she get enough money together to escape? And that was the promise she had made herself. She was going to get home and see her family again. A rush of longing pulled at Roza's insides.

Working at Rainbow would get her off to a good start, but she had to face it, even when she'd saved up enough, she couldn't simply hop on a plane to Albania. She didn't have her passport for one thing. And if Aunty Sade found out she was coming back she might have men in her pay who would stop her at Tirana... it didn't bear thinking about. There was only one way she could return home safely. She had to find the man Mrs Cicu had told her about.

Now that she had decided to accept the job, Roza was impatient to start. But she had not reckoned on the night terrors which descended out of nowhere. Locked in the dirty cupboard, gasping for air, with no Jozif to pull her out – only Adelina opening the door and then closing it again, toying with her. Trying to wake up was like fighting through a tunnel of thickets. One day drifted into another.

Roza could barely summon up enough energy to make the beds and prepare the meals. It was only when she burned the sausages and set off the fire alarm that Jozif intervened, sending Roza to her room before Adelina could get to her.

'She is recovering, Adelina. You must give her time,' she heard him say.

That weekend the family went to Legoland. Alone in the house, Roza slept all day. She was woken by Mr Pam's motorbike phut-phutting into the drive as he returned home from work.

Over a week had passed since her day at *Rainbow*. What if Wendy thought she was spurning her offer and had found someone else?

Wendy didn't seem at all surprised to see her. 'Ooh, that's colourful.' She admired Roza's new t-shirt with its rainbow motif.

It had been at the bottom of the clothes bag. And though it hung on her like a sack, the long sleeves hid what was left of the marks on her arms.

'Third week of June already.' Wendy ran her finger down the rota. 'How about Mondays and Wednesdays? Easier for me if you can manage regular days.'

Roza nodded with enthusiasm. Better for her too.

'There may be extra shifts, if you're interested.' Wendy pulled out a green file from under the counter. 'I'm going to need some ID from you, lovey. Passport would be best.'

Roza looked at her blankly. 'Um . . . we have just moved here. It is a bit . . . er, difficult to find . . . at the moment.'

Her face was heating up but it was the truth. She had spent an hour the day before trying to locate it.

Wendy snapped the file shut and gave Carla a quick sideways glance. 'Let me have it when you can,' she said quietly. 'It's not like you'll be doing more than a few hours a week.'

She turned to talk to Carla about the milk order.

Roza let her eyes drift to the wall next to the window. A new painting had appeared. A turquoise sea, boats bobbing on the surface, the sky smudged with pink. It wasn't the one her teacher had pinned to the classroom wall but the style was similar. If she stared at it for long enough the journalist's name might come back to her.

'I like that one too,' Wendy said over her shoulder. 'Jason put it up yesterday to replace the one he sold. Don't ask me what it's called though, I'm no Picasso!'

'Did he paint it?'

'Yes.' Wendy rolled her eyes. 'Funny how he finds time to do the things he enjoys!'

The boy who could not be bothered to turn up for work on time, or even at all some days, according to Wendy. Roza should probably be thanking this Jason. If he wasn't so unreliable Wendy might not have given her the job.

'Oh, here we go!' Wendy's phone tinkled with an incoming message. 'I was going to say we'll ask him about that picture. Not today though.' She held out her phone.

Job Centre just rang. Interview @ 11. Sorry Aunty Wend.

Chapter Sixteen

Roza flicked the switch on the kettle and measured out the rounded spoonful of coffee Wendy liked in her *Boss Lady* mug.

Two whole weeks had gone by. And nothing had happened to stop her turning up for her shifts. It was a miracle!

Cautiously she flexed her neck. It stung too much to turn it properly to the right after the shaking Adelina had given her the night before.

I must have slept awkwardly, she said when Wendy commented.

She had stood her ground with Adelina though – she was proud of that – countering Madam with a laser-eyed look of her own.

She had been thinking a lot about what Jozif had said. *Bad blood*. So her father had fallen out with his niece years ago. That explained why Roza had only that one memory of Adelina. And the jibes Madam made about Babi. Most of them anyway. Not *Frikacak*. Coward. What was that about? It wasn't Roza's fault they had never made up. And if the sight of her in their home made the woman unhappy, why had she agreed for Roza to move in?

Think about something else!

Working at *Rainbow* was a world away from her life in Ridley Road and that was how she wanted to keep it.

A little square of sunshine glowed just beyond the back door. Roza stepped outside. There was someone in the shed. A boy, talking.

She didn't see him properly until the phone tucked under his chin dropped with a clunk on to the paving stones.

He pointed his finger at her. 'You must be the Worker Bee. Gettin' me into trouble with the boss.'

She couldn't believe it. It was the boy on the bike. The one who had stopped to talk to her when she was sitting like a collapsed blancmange in the lane. *That* day!

'I'm the lazy drone, by the way.' He blew the dust off his phone and turned it over, inspecting it for damage. 'Wendy's got a bit of a thing about bees.'

'You are Jason?'

The kettle came to the boil. Roza hurried back inside.

'I'll have a cup if you're making one for the boss,' he called after her. 'Two sugars, please.'

He hadn't recognised *her* though. That was a relief.

Roza raised her eyes to the window as she stirred milk into Wendy's mug. Every few minutes he stopped to hoist his jeans up at the back. And was that the line of his pants showing? *Calvin Klein.* He hadn't stopped jabbering on his phone the whole time she'd been standing there. *Greg this and Josh that!* She had never known a boy with so much to say.

He wiped his hands on his jeans and stepped inside. Now he was standing close up, she could see he was a good head taller than her and with thick arms. Like his nose and cheeks, they were covered in freckles.

'Is that coffee?' Wendy had come up behind Roza. 'Oh . . .'

'How you doing, Aunty Wend?' The boy pulled off his beanie and stepped forward to plant a kiss on her cheek.

Wendy swatted him away and folded her arms across her chest. 'Pah! Don't think you can get round me, Jason White.'

But her lips were twitching. 'And for heaven's sake, give me those jeans to take up. Don't you know what a sight you look?'

Jason pulled a face at her retreating back and reached his hand into the biscuit barrel. 'So, where you from Roza? OK if I call you Ro?'

'No! Roza is my name. I am from Albania.'

Could she have sounded more pompous? She busied herself scraping out one of the big salad bowls and flicked the hot tap on ready to wash it out.

'So, what's your story? I bet Wendy's told you mine.' His grin revealed a row of uneven teeth.

Her story? Exchanging just a few words with this boy was enough to make Roza feel like she had swallowed a pile of jumping beans.

Back in Albania she and Stefanie had talked about boys in the UK.

'It will be different there.' Her friend flashed one of her full-on, know-it-all smiles. 'Where you are going, girls are more forward. Hey, you can kiss a boy in the street without your father grounding you for a week.'

Kiss a boy? Boys were a no-no until she was eighteen or nineteen. Her father had made that clear. And this Jason was clearly unreliable into the bargain. Though it had been sweet of him to stop and ask her what was wrong that day; offer to buy her a hot drink. He had a cute face too, and the way his tongue was chasing biscuit crumbs around his lips was making her insides tingle.

What was she thinking? She had no space in her life for a boyfriend or any boy, come to that. *Trust yourself, Roza, no one else.*

She checked herself. She was in the middle of doing something. Yes, washing up. She plunged her right hand into the sink. 'Aargh.' The water was steaming and ready to overflow.

'You OK?' Jason shot off the stool and pulling the plug spun the cold tap to full. He grabbed her hand. 'Now keep it there, right? Till it stops burning.'

She nodded and screwed up her face, turning her head so he wouldn't see her tears.

'Trust me.' He launched into a story about how he had burned his arm pulling an uninflated balloon out of a fire when he was ten. He turned it over to show her. There was a pale indented circle on the underside. 'Wild, eh? Even the scar's balloon-shaped.'

When was he going to let go of her hand? Outside of her family, she had never stood so close to a boy. She could feel the solidness of him, smell the sweet woody soap he'd washed with that morning. She tilted her head a few degrees. His eyes were green. That was a surprise.

She prised her hand away. 'Thank you,' she said. The pain was easing. Not much, but enough for her to put on a brave face.

'I've seen you somewhere,' he said slowly. 'Your face looks—'

'So, Wendy is your aunty?' Roza cut in.

'Yeah, kind of.' He was still looking at her, his eyes moving in a weird way.

'And you live with her?' She was running out of things to say. Surely it was time for him to get back to unloading boxes from the shed?

Her question triggered only another story. About his grandfather this time, who had emigrated from Trinidad in the 1960s. 'He fell for a white girl, ended up marrying her. Thirty years later my Dad and his brother did the same, only by then it was the nineties so most people were cool with that. Not everyone, mind. It caused a right ruckus in Wendy's family.'

He was still going at ninety miles an hour when Wendy crashed in.

'If you want a bed for the night Jason White, you'd better stop distracting Roza and get a move on. I'm paying both of you to work here, remember!' She hefted the bowl of clean dishes against her stomach and clomped off.

Roza grimaced. 'Did she mean what she said? It wasn't your fault...'

'Don't stress about it,' Jason helped himself to another biscuit. 'She threatens to throw me out at least once a week.'

Chapter Seventeen

IT WAS HER FIRST visit to the library since that dreadful day at the end of May.

Roza couldn't settle to her books no matter how many times she rearranged them. The news headlines might have changed but that didn't stop her thinking about the slave girl. Did she get home to Romania? Were her family happy to take her back?

How long would it take *Roza* to escape?

In four weeks she'd already saved up over one hundred pounds. A quarter of the way to her target. She'd put half of the money in a plastic bag and hooked it to the back of the washing machine. The rest was safely concealed in the secret pocket of her backpack. She smiled to herself. Stefanie would be pleased to know she was putting it to good use.

As soon as she'd reached four hundred pounds she'd head for London. Where that man lived – the one Mrs Cicu had told her about. She pressed her fingers against her temples. What else could she remember about him? Besides the fact that he was a journalist and a *good man*.

There had been something about his name, something that had surprised her. Roza squeezed her eyes shut, concentrating hard. Yes! It was the same as the artist of that amazing painting. If only she could remember *that* name.

She shook her head, still cross with herself that she'd not seen that little blue card with his name and address for what it was at the time. A lifeline.

Mr Joe perched on the edge of the table, swinging his left leg back and forth. 'Hello! Haven't seen you in here for a while. How's it going at *Rainbow*?'

'Good, thank you. Wendy is very kind.'

'Still not made up your mind what to do?'

It took Roza a moment to work out what he was talking about. The little speech Adelina expected her to give. Deciding what to do with her future.

She shook her head.

He glanced down at the book she was reading. *The Nineteenth Century Slave Trade in Europe.* 'That looks heavy going,' he said.

He left her to it and went to help someone having trouble with one of the computers.

Roza sat back and imagined the word as Aunty Sade might say it, rolling her 'r's. *SLAVERRRY.* If Roza told Aunty she was a modern slave she would tell her not to talk such nonsense. She would tell her niece how *grateful* she should be.

Roza clapped the book shut. It would be easier not to bother with her studies at all but that would mean Sade and Adelina had won.

Women need education, Roza. Work hard at your studies, so when you are grown up you can get a job you love.

Mrs Cicu. She had been so much more than just a teacher. Giving Roza extra lessons at home, letting her and Stefanie use the internet for research. She had even taken Mami in her car to visit Sindi's grave.

You could be a teacher too, Roza.

Little chance of that now, Mrs Cicu.

There was a computer free. Roza typed the phrase *modern slavery* into the search box and leaned towards the screen.

So it wasn't only about being locked up in a house and denied an education. Her stomach churned as she read one report after another. Babies stolen for adoption, boys made to work in cannabis farms, people forced to give up their kidneys for organ transplants.

Her eyes landed on another headline. *Young girls sold as cargo into the sex trade.*

Cargo? The word Aunty Sade had used on the phone. Was *that* what her business in Tirana was about – people trafficking? And the Dori woman on the plane, she must be involved too.

A sudden horrible thought came back to her. The maid at Aunty Sade's house. She was a slave too, wasn't she?

It was all starting to make sense.

Roza wiped her clammy hands against her jeans. She had to find somewhere where she could think.

As she passed the returns trolley, Mr Joe stopped her. 'You can tell me to mind my own business,' he said. 'But whenever you come here, I get the feeling something's not right. I couldn't help noticing how you rushed out last time.'

The walls felt like they were pressing in. How close did she have to get for the automatic doors to open?

'There are places you can ring, you know. For help.' He tapped a noticeboard on the wall. Among the posters – Rape Crisis, Domestic Abuse – there was one of a girl holding up a piece of card: **SOLD.**

Roza thought back to the policeman – he had seemed kind and look how that ended. She forced herself to look at Mr Joe. 'I am fine, thank you,' she muttered.

The doors slid open. A mousy-looking woman stepped in, shaking the rain from her umbrella. 'Sorry I'm late, Joe. The buses.' She rolled her eyes.

Roza shot out before he had a chance to say any more.

The next day she arrived at *Rainbow* to find Wendy poring over a rota. It had lots of gaps and crossed-out names.

'If I give the other girls too many shifts, they lose money on their benefits.'

'I can work Friday afternoon,' Roza said on an impulse. Adelina was taking the boys shopping for new shoes after school.

'You sure, lovey?' Wendy didn't wait for an answer. She was already writing her name in the blank space. 'It's a good job you and Jason can slot in when I need you.'

'Is he doing extra shifts too?' Roza's stomach did a little skip.

So far they had worked three days together and already he was starting to feel like a friend. As long as she could keep dodging his awkward questions about her family and home life.

Jason was still on her mind when Wendy sent her to the 8-til-late after lunch. His snag-toothed smile, the way he greeted her – *Good Morning, Miss Albania. – always looking her in the eye. It was one of the things she liked most about him.* Perhaps in time he was someone she could trust, confide in?

She shook herself. She enjoyed working with him; he made her laugh. Trusting him with her secret was another matter.

She lifted two cartons of milk from the fridge and looked around for the seeded bread Wendy liked.

'What you doing here, *budalla*?'

Skender! Her heart began thumping like a drumbeat. 'As you see, I am . . . buying groceries for your mother,' she said.

His face blanked. Only for a second though. He pulled his earbuds out. 'Nice try. *Tut tut.* You're not supposed to be out of the house.'

She clenched her free hand digging her nails into her palm. 'And you should be at school,' she hissed.

'Can't tell my mother though, can you?'

'Can't I?'

She forced herself to hold his gaze. His brazenness had knocked the breath out of her. How was this going to play out?

'You can do me and my mates a favour. Grumpy Grandma down there won't sell us any fags but you can get us a bag of those posh chocolates.' He nodded towards a display tub at the top of the next aisle. 'Bring them outside.'

'Steal them? I will not do that!'

'You know who I'll be telling,' he added in a sing-song voice.

Roza watched him swagger down the aisle like a gangster. He muttered something to the woman behind the till.

Should she call his bluff? She sighed. It wasn't worth the risk.

A bell rang as Roza scanned the aisles and the only assistant she could see, who'd been stocking the fridge with yogurts, hurried to the front of the shop.

Roza ambled towards the chocolates and picked up a bag, pretending to study the ingredients. When she was sure there was no one around, she tucked it inside her coat.

At the till, she imagined the word *THIEF* branded across her forehead in large letters but when she handed over the money for the bread and milk the young assistant barely looked up to give her the change.

Skender and his friends were waiting in the loading bay. She recognised the bigger boy from the shoe scuffle a few weeks before. He looked her up and down and sniggered. 'Nice one, Sken.'

He was old enough that his voice was breaking.

'You make a habit to hang around with the infants' class?' Roza gave him the gimlet eye and thrust the chocolates at Skender.

'Bitch,' the older boy called as she walked away.

Roza took a sideways glance at *Rainbow*. Now she had to pretend she was heading for the road back to Thornley. She only hoped Wendy wasn't looking out of the window.

Chapter Eighteen

Roza tipped the slab of mince into the pan and stabbed it with more force than necessary. How could she have let Skender, a thirteen-year-old boy intimidate her like that? When she'd eventually slipped back inside *Rainbow*, Wendy told her she could have milked a cow she had been gone so long.

Roza wasn't going to let him do that to her again.

The front door of the house flew open, as though a sudden gust of wind had caught it.

'*Skender!*'

Roza jumped. Adelina was never home this early.

She counted to ten in her head, the time it usually took Madam to reach the top of the stairs. Right on cue a crash reverberated through the house. She pictured the scene – Skender's Xbox flying across the room in the melee of muffled cries and furious shouting.

Roza crept to the foot of the stairs and then a couple of steps higher. Skender's door was half-open, giving her a good view of Adelina's broad back.

'Someone took film of you swearing at the shop assistant and sent it to your head teacher, you stupid boy. I have seen it too. Don't deny it.'

Was that what had happened before Skender pounced? Had *she* been caught on camera too?

'It wasn't my idea. The others pick on me all the time, I've told you that.'

'And you think your father is going to believe that when he finds out? *It is Brighton all over again*, that is what he says to me. And it is true Skender. Smoking, detentions, now this!'

'He hates me anyway. Never comes to sports days or anything like that.' Skender sniffed.

There was a long pause. He was crying properly now.

'He wants to send you to that boarding school we looked at.'

'He can't make me! I'll run away!' The ceiling rattled. Skender must have jumped off the bed. 'Those places are full of bullies. Manny's cousin was tied up with parcel tape and dunked in the river.'

'Then you had better make sure your behaviour improves. I am running out of excuses for you.'

Roza slipped back to the kitchen. She'd heard enough.

After supper was over, Jozif and Adelina went out for a drink with some people Jozif worked with. Roza left Albi in the bath playing with the bubble blower and waited until the car was out of sight.

Balling her fists, she flung open Skender's door. 'Never ask me to steal for you again. Or I will make sure Jozif finds out that you are not only skiving off school and harassing people, you are stealing as well.'

Skender's face blanched. *He wasn't expecting that. Good!* She pulled the door behind her before he had time to find his tongue.

Anger was still pumping through her. Roza sat down on the bathroom floor to give herself a moment. Slowly, her heart rate steadied. She took the bubble-blower from Albi and with a long, steady breath, produced one the size of a grapefruit. Albi screamed with delight as it bounced softly off the tiles.

'Time to come out.' Roza turned to the heated rail behind her. Albi's Thomas the Tank Engine towel must still be in the tumble dryer. 'Keep blowing, Albi. I'll only be a second,' she said.

She raced downstairs and squatted in front of the dryer. As she pulled Albi's towel free from the tangle of clothes a scream rang out upstairs.

'Albi?' She took the stairs two at a time. A quick glance in Skender's room confirmed her worst fears.

Roza threw herself at the bathroom door, banging hard with her fists.

'Open the door, Skender. I know you're in there.'

What was he up to?

He could be horrible to his little brother, teasing and taunting him and hiding Roo. But surely he wouldn't harm Albi himself?

Suddenly the picture forming in Roza's head was more than she could bear. .

'Stop it! Stop whatever you are doing to him!'

Albi was retching and spluttering, his legs kicking the side of the bath. Water was sloshing onto the floor.

She carried on pounding at the door – her fists sore, her face wet with furious tears.

Finally, Skender released the lock. Albi's hair was plastered to his head, snot running into his mouth. Roza scooped the little boy up in the towel and, gripping him against her, crooned into his ear.

Skender held up his hands. A small smile played around his lips. 'He slipped under. Good job I was here. Shouldn't have left him, should you? Don't know what my mother would say if she found out.'

Chapter Nineteen

'Yeah mate, let's book it soon.'

Jason emerged from the shed with an overloaded trolley, his phone tucked under his chin. 'Whoops!'

Catching a slipping tin of beans, he beamed his easy smile at Roza. 'Morning, Miss Albania.'

Roza scowled at him. 'Who are you talking to now? You are always on the phone.'

'Ouch! Just Greg.' He pulled a face. 'You a'right? What you been up to that's made you so grumpy?'

What have I been up to? Nothing much – just being blackmailed by a thirteen-year-old, then letting him half-drown his little brother. And now I'm worried he's going to tell his mother it was all my fault. No, nothing much at all!

'Roza?' Jason put a hand on her arm. She needed to calm down.

She angled her head and forced out her own smile. 'Sorry. It's nothing.' She took a breath. 'Now, tell me what you are planning with *Greg*.'

'Getting ready to hit the surf!' Jason made a wave-like movement with his hand. 'Can't wait.' He parked the trolley and strolled back out to the shed, whistling.

Roza went back to filling the dishwasher. Almost a week had passed. If Skender had said anything to his mother, Roza was sure to have known about it by now. In the meantime, she was doing her best to keep Albi safe. The little boy was terrified of being left on his own with his big brother and – she had no doubt about this – what he had threatened if Albi told on him. She was desperate to talk it through with someone. But she couldn't. Could she?

Jason reappeared with the stepladder.

'What's this then?' He pulled out the biography of Queen Victoria poking from her backpack and read the blurb. 'Hot stuff!'

He lifted a palette of tinned peaches on to the top of the ladder and started to climb. 'I don't get it. If you like studying so much, how come you dropped out of school?'

'I did not drop out.' Roza huffed and rubbed furiously at the hob where the soup had boiled over.

'What then? Your parents won't let you stay on?' He unloaded the tins on to the shelf and frowned at her. 'Please don't tell me it's cos you're a girl? That kind of thinking went out with the ark.'

Roza chewed the inside of her mouth. What was she supposed to say to that?

'OK, I get it. MYOB Jase. Mind your own beeswax, as my dad used to say.'

'Did you really say *beeswax*?' She couldn't help giggling. Another phrase to look up.

'Beeswax. Business. Get it?'

She rinsed out the scouring pad. 'My family are very . . . traditional. About where I go, what I do, who I spend time with. They do not know I am working here. When I am older, I intend to leave home and work in London.'

'I don't blame you. No wonder you're in a grump if they treat you like that.' Jason climbed down to fetch another palette.

'Well, you won't have any trouble getting a job. Your English is better than mine.'

Roza laughed. 'Hardly, but I had a very good teacher.' She dried her hands and looked at him. 'So why did *you* leave school?'

'Waste of time. Didn't want to be there.'

'What about the course you're doing now? Not your *cup of tea*?'

It was Jason's turn to laugh. 'Nice one.' He puffed his cheeks and blew out. 'Travel and Tourism? Only chose it cos it looked easy.'

'So what *would* you like to do? Apart from being a professional surfer?'

'Haha. I wish!' Jason climbed down and snapped the stepladder closed. 'Dunno yet. Ambulance driver, paramedic? Something practical, y'know. I'd be useless sitting at a desk all day.'

'You will need to take exams.'

'Yeah. I'll have to, y'know, find out.'

'You should do that,' Roza said with emphasis. 'Education is most important.'

By the following week the paintings had changed again.

After a slow morning, the cafe was almost empty. Roza dragged a cloth over the table Jason had just cleared and turned her attention to the display wall. The seascape scene that had caught her eye when she first started was back – pink cliffs, boats bobbing on the foam.

Jason dumped the dirty plates on the hatch and came to stand next to her. 'Do you like it?' He rubbed gently at a small smudge on the glass.

'Wendy said they are your paintings.'

'Yeah, but they're not my own.' He gave her a lopsided grin.

'Now you are confusing me.'

'I copy other people's paintings. Famous artists. Our art teacher told us to paint something in the style of Renoir. I cheated. Found one that wasn't so well-known and copied it. Miss Wilson was well impressed. She didn't have a clue. My mum asked me to do one for her friend after that and it all went from there. Just got the knack, I guess. Makes me a bit of spare cash.' He winked at her. 'Enough to buy my own surfboard.'

'*This* picture reminds me of another painting. One I really liked,' Roza said. 'I think there were fishing boats in that too.'

The same strong feeling was coming over her that if she let these colours burn into her brain for long enough, the full memory of that afternoon with Mrs Cicu would come back. And she'd remember the man's name.

'I've done loads. Come round and take a look the others if you want.'

Roza checked the clock above the coffee machine. They were closing early. Wendy was visiting her neighbour who had just moved into a care home.

Wendy's neat bungalow was on the same road as the library. There were lace curtains at the windows, a pebbled driveway lined with pots of petunias and a front door decorated with wooden bumblebees.

Roza shuffled inside. It didn't feel right being at Wendy's when she wasn't there herself. And now she was going upstairs with a boy. What would Babi say?

She hovered in the doorway while Jason tugged his curtains back and pushed open a window. 'Sorry. It's a bit rank in here.'

There was a rucksack in the corner with t-shirts and a wetsuit spilling out of the mouth. On the bed, boxer shorts and a pair of jeans. Was he going away so soon?

There were no chairs, so Roza perched on the edge of the bed and switched her attention to the two pencil drawings above it. 'Is that you?'

'Yeah, me on the left. Then me and my mum in the other. My dad did them.'

Jason drew out a large square box from underneath the bed and wiped the dust off the top with a corner of the duvet. 'I've never shown anyone before. Most of these are pretty rough.'

'I'm not going to laugh, if that's what you think,' Roza said.

He lifted out the picture on top. Flowers springing from the top of a brown vase.

Jason snorted. 'Ugh! I can't believe I've kept all these! A few of them were up in the library before Wendy said I could sell them in the cafe.'

Several pictures later, he uncovered the one she'd been waiting for – a corkscrew of sunlight on still water, the black stalks of the boatmen. A copy of the painting her brain had been struggling to summon up all these months. Doing her best to control the tremor in her hand, she reached across Jason and edged it out.

'Monet's *Sunrise*,' Jason said matter-of-factly. He had scribbled the artist's name at the bottom.

So the *t* was silent.

My sister Juliana's husband. If ever you should be in need...

Roza jumped up. 'Can I take the picture? I will pay you for it.'

'Is that the one you've been on about? It's not very good. It was one of my first.'

For a moment, Roza was afraid he wouldn't let her have it. She counted five pound coins out of her pocket and placed them in a pile on the little cupboard next to the bed.

Jason shrugged. 'Oh. Well, OK then.'

She lifted the painting by the corners, holding it like it was a piece of porcelain.

Jason said, 'You don't have to go yet, do you?'

She nodded. It must be after three. Adelina had been in a surprisingly good mood all week and there had been no mention of Albi's fright in the bath, but she would still expect the upstairs windows to be gleaming when she got home. So far Roza had only managed the boys' rooms.

She shifted her feet. The way he was looking at her, his green eyes so dark and serious for once, was making her uneasy.

He picked up a folded sheet of paper from his bedside cupboard. When he opened it up, he frowned at the tight curly writing before putting it down on the bed. 'There was something I wanted to show you at the park, that's all. 'Bout my grandad.'

'Was he the one who died? Wendy told me your mother had to move into a care home...'

Jason's face folded like she'd hit him.

'Sorry I've got to...' Roza stepped back and reached behind her for the doorknob.

He dumped the paintings back into the box and rammed the lid on. His gaze had shifted to the floor. He stood up and hooked his thumbs through his belt loops. 'It's... cool. We can do it another time.'

That night Roza spread the *Sunrise* painting across the couch. The thrill it gave her the first time she had seen it flooded back, reconnecting her with Mrs Cicu... with her life in Albania. Something inside lifted, filling her with warmth and peace.

Mr Monet. The journalist. A good man.

Chapter Twenty

'How was Jason when you saw him last, lovey?'

It was the first thing Wendy said when Roza turned up that Friday.

Roza had thought twice before agreeing to do an extra shift. Adelina was still piling on the chores. But she needed the money for her escape. She'd just have to work double quick cleaning the bathroom and the Brakas en suite when she got back.

She looked up. Wendy was waiting for an answer.

'Um,' Roza cast her mind back. Did Wendy know she had been at her house the week before? 'All right, I think,' she said.

'He's gone away,' Wendy said. 'He didn't come home Wednesday night. Said he was staying with his friend. Then he sent me a text yesterday. Something about needing to get away; get some *head space*.' She made speech marks with her fingers.

Roza felt sorry for Wendy. And cross with Jason. He could have told one of them where he was going and when he'd be back.

They worked in silence for most of the shift. Then ten minutes before closing time, Wendy came through to the kitchen.

'His grandad's anniversary,' she said. 'That'll be it. It's about a year now since he passed on. Jason doesn't let on much but they were very close after his dad died.'

Roza pulled a plate from the dishwasher. It was coming back to her now. Jason *hadn't* been OK. She'd been so preoccupied about finding the painting and getting back to Ridley Road she hadn't taken much notice.

She was home before two. Today she needed to scour the shower tiles and bleach the grouting.

When she stood down from the step stool her arms ached; her back too. And there was still the en suite in Adelina and Jozif's bedroom to tackle.

Downstairs, she filled a glass from the tap. Her backpack was on the couch in her cell. She must put it out of sight before Skender came home. Secret pocket or not, she didn't want him nosing around.

She'd counted her money again yesterday. At this rate, with the extra shifts Wendy had promised, she'd be ready to leave for London in six or seven weeks at the most. Only one thing was stopping her. Finding out Mr Monet's email or his home address.

Her visit to the library earlier that morning had been brief and fruitless. The only other Monet outside all the websites dedicated to the artist – and there was no end of those - was a furniture designer in Manhattan. Had Roza remembered the journalist's name correctly?

A key turned in the front door, startling her. Jozif. His tired features told of a bad day. He swept past her without so much as a glance and laid his briefcase on the table.

'I passed you on the main road for Marwood this morning on my way to a house call,' he said. His mouth was tight. 'If Adelina discovers you are going out . . .'

'Are you going to tell her?' Roza drained her glass of water, surprised at how calm she felt.

'Of course not. I released the catch on the window to allow you to leave the house for short periods; use the garden.'

'It is not enough,' said Roza. 'Not any more. I have been . . .'

'Stop!' His hand flew up. 'I do not wish to know where you go or what you do. I am telling you this for your own good. If you make more trouble for Adelina, she will get rid of you and that will be far worse.'

'What do you mean, *get rid of* me?' Roza's skin prickled.

'Better to not find out.'

'I want to know!' She banged the glass down on the counter. 'Tell me why she hates me so much; hates my father. Something happened between them many years ago. What was it? It's my family too. I'm entitled to know.'

Shaking his head, he muttered something.

'*The sins of the father?* What does that mean?'

'I can put it no other way. Adelina still blames Arben for her father's death.'

'Blame? Why, what happened?' Uncle Vasil had died before Roza was born. She had no idea how. It had never been mentioned at home.

'There was an accident. Your father was driving. The car ended up in a lake and everyone except Arben died.'

Roza bumped down on to a kitchen chair. 'Was Babi arrested?'

'Charges were never brought. The police decided he was young and inexperienced. And Vasil – well, let's just say that your father was only on the golfing trip to drive the other men. So they could enjoy their drinking.'

A picture was forming in Roza's head. Babi thrashing around in the water. Men trapped in the car.

Jozif carried on talking. 'You need to understand, my wife was a young girl. Her life took a terrible downturn after her father died.'

'Stop making excuses for her! *I* have done nothing wrong. Why do you let her treat me like this? You are a doctor! You should be protecting me.'

'Sade has power in Albania which she would use against my family there if I left Adelina. *And* she would make sure I never saw Albi again.'

'Or Skender?'

'Skender is not my child.'

Roza went back to cleaning the en suite. She couldn't stop thinking about her father – not much older than her, eager to please his powerful brother-in-law, unable to say no to chauffeuring him and his friends.

What if he had driven recklessly? Or been drunk himself?

A few months ago she wouldn't have thought twice about defending Babi. But he was no longer the man she thought he was.

Adelina's people carrier hummed into the driveway as Roza was finishing. She poured bleach down the toilet. Madam would like that – the clinical smell it gave off.

Downstairs, Albi ran through the front door and up to Roza, Roo tucked under his arm. He buried his face between her legs, wanting to know where Skender was. She settled him in front of the TV with a drink and a biscuit and pulled out the chopping board to make a start on supper. Above her, Adelina was padding about. Checking the en suite, no doubt.

As she chopped the vegetables, an idea took shape in Roza's head. Even though it was a long time ago, she could tell Adelina how sorry she was about Uncle Vasil's death; how hard it must have been for her. That Babi would be upset to know how much it had affected her. Adults used words like that, to comfort people who were grieving.

'Roza! Come upstairs.'

She turned the heat off under the frying onions. Adelina had used her name! Should she take that as a good sign?

In the hall, she almost ran into Skender. He stood in her way pulling silly faces. 'Splish splash,' he whispered, an ugly smile filling his face.

'Roza! Are you coming?'

She shoved him aside – he was still small enough to do that – and raced up the stairs.

Adelina was in the en suite.

Roza's hands felt clammy. She rubbed them down the sides of her jeans. 'Come in, come in.' Adelina beckoned her. 'I wanted to compliment you on

working so hard in here. It smells good.

It was a squeeze, the two of them in such a confined space. Adelina was bigger than ever and her cloying scent was catching in Roza's throat.

'I . . . I wanted to say . . .' Roza squeezed her hands together.
Go on.

'Yes?' Adelina was actually looking at her, waiting.

Sorryforhowyourfatherdied. The words froze on Roza's lips.

'Oh look, there is one small mark you have missed on the mirror.' Adelina handed her a cloth.

Roza stretched across in front of her. She couldn't see any smears.

Adelina stiffened. 'Having trouble getting the words out?'

Slowly her hands rose in the mirror circling Roza's head like a bird of prey. Then she dug her nails into Roza's scalp, forcing her down towards the toilet pan – only her head was too big and her forehead was clunking against the sides. Again and again, Adelina yanked the flush, as though she just couldn't get rid of this piece of waste. When Roza tried to scream, the bleached water cascaded into her mouth.

Finally, Adelina's hands loosened. She yanked Roza up by her ponytail

'*Sorry.* Was that what you wanted to say, *budalla*? Sorry for leaving my son on his own so that he nearly drowned? This will teach you not to take better care of him.'

She rinsed her hands under the tap and dried them on the towel.

'Now, clean yourself up. And get supper on the table!'

Chapter Twenty-One

ROZA RANG THE CAFE on Monday lunchtime when she knew Wendy wouldn't have time to answer. She left a message. Wendy wouldn't want her there anyway. Not with a stomach upset – and that was close enough to the truth.

The bad dreams and rigors were back, stealing Roza's strength from her and leaving her to stumble through each day. This wouldn't last, it was just a setback. She *would* get away; see her family again. She had to keep telling herself that. But she didn't know how much more she could take.

The following Monday, she found an old tube of Adelina's make-up and smoothed it over the bruise on her forehead. She was determined not to miss any more shifts. It wasn't just about not letting Wendy down – every pound meant one more step towards freedom.

When Roza arrived, Wendy tilted her head to ask how she was. 'You still look a bit peaky,' she said.

Roza mumbled that she was fine and pulled her apron off the hook.

'This turned up today.' Wendy held out a postcard. An endless stretch of white sand and sea. On the back, a three-line message written in a scratchy pen. *Hi Aunty Wend, I'm here in Bournemouth! With Greg and Josh. Surf's up! Nothing to worry about. See you soon.* He had drawn a smiley face at the bottom and added three kisses.

Roza gave Wendy a stiff nod and handed it back. So much for going away to grieve for his grandad. She should have guessed from the wetsuit poking out of his rucksack.

She wrenched open the dishwasher. She had more important things to think about than Jason and his selfish teenage-boy behaviour. And to think she had been hoping he was someone she could trust and confide in one day.

Wendy gave her a funny look. 'You really don't look yourself.'

'I'm OK.' Roza's throat was thick. If she was going to get through her shift, the last thing she needed was Wendy feeling sorry for her. She turned to pick up the bowl of dirty plates Carla had left on the hatch.

'Everything all right at home, is it?' Wendy's voice was quiet *Please go away.*

'I'll leave you to it then.'

The morning dragged. The cafe was quieter than Roza had ever known it. There were lots of empty tables and too much time to think.

Wendy and Mr Joe sat together talking at his usual window table. As Roza came through with her own lunch their heads were together, their faces solemn like someone had died. As he saw her, Mr Joe managed a half-smile. But he looked ill at ease.

She pushed her hands into her pockets. A few more weeks and she'd be on her way. She just had to keep her head down and hope nothing else went wrong.

Chapter Twenty-Two

THE NEXT WEEK, ROZA was allowed out to take Albi to holiday club at the leisure centre.

As she said goodbye and hooked his scooter over her arm, she couldn't help thinking of Ylli. How would Mami keep him occupied this summer now that Roza wasn't there to take him to the lake?

On the way out, a flyer for an open day at Marwood College caught her eye. Two boys and a girl. The girl wore her hair in a French plait, in the same way Mami used to do hers. All three of them were grinning into the camera with their polished faces and perfect teeth. *Lucky kids, going to college.*

Roza's mind flipped to the conversation with Jason. Was he serious about becoming a paramedic? Or just saying it to impress her?

It was early enough that there were several computers free at the library. She typed in the web address for the college and clicked on the link for A-level courses. *Paramedic training – Qualifications and qualities.* She ran her eyes down the list. *Strong communication skills.* Jason was certainly a good talker. *Empathy and care for others.* She'd have to think about that one. He'd been kind to her but he'd let Wendy down, staying away for weeks.

Roza copied the link for the course into the blank space at the foot of the flyer and tucked it into her pocket. It was hard to imagine Jason doing anything about it. He'd probably roll his eyes, tell her to MYOB. Still, no harm in giving him a push in the right direction. He had to come back to Thornley sometime.

The hot weather held. Adelina was at work all week. She left written instructions for Roza to take Albi to the park on the far side of Marwood where there was children's entertainment every afternoon.

On Thursday, Skender pulled up on his bike. At first he was keen to play with Albi, helping him work his way across the monkey bars on the small climbing frame. But it wasn't long before his friends arrived – running up the slides and getting in the way of the younger kids. When one of the mothers, a tall woman with a commanding voice, stepped in and told them to find somewhere else to play, Skender swore at her and sloped off towards the trees with the others.

The magic show started soon after that – thank goodness. Roza made sure to find a spot in the middle of the crowd well out of Skender's way. As the show finished, he was still sitting cross-legged with the older boy at the edge of the wood. The smell of weed drifted across with the breeze.

Roza pulled Albi in the opposite direction. 'Come on,' she said. 'Race you to the gate.'

At least both boys would be away at Jozif's sister's for the final week of the holidays, leaving her free to slip out and work at *Rainbow*. The last thing she wanted was any more trouble with Skender.

***

On Friday morning she was roused by thundery rain. It hit the ground like firecrackers and glug-glugged into the drain below her window.

'We'll have to walk,' she said, helping Albi put on his wellies.

'Don't want to go.'

'It's the last day, you'll have fun.'

Roza wasn't in the mood to humour him. She'd been woken by Adelina's shrieks late the night before. Then lain rigid for an hour waiting for Adelina to crash into her cell and take Skender's sins out on her.

They were nearly at the leisure centre when Albi started up again. 'Don't want to go. Want Roo.' He stopped dead in the middle of the pavement, tears rolling down his cheeks.

She crouched down in front of him, willing herself to be patient. At least the rain was easing.

'Hey, Ro! Roza, it *is* you, isn't it?'

Jason was standing on the opposite pavement, waving.

She straightened up as he bounded across the road.

'He looks like man on CBeebies.' Albi's face brightened. He dragged a hand across his nose and beamed up at Jason.

'Hey, who's this? What's your name, little guy?' Jason held his hand up for a high five.

Roza glared at him. It was bad enough that he'd gone away without telling her, now he was behaving as though nothing had happened and making her heart do those little skips.

'Come on Albi, we'll be late.' She tugged at the little boy's hand. She didn't want Albi mentioning *Roza's friend* to his mother. 'And we don't talk to strangers, do we?'

***

It was no surprise to find Jason waiting outside the leisure centre.

He pushed his hands deep into his pockets. 'Will he tell your dad?'

Roza shrugged.

'And you'll be in trouble. Sorry Ro, but you can't blame me for being pleased to see you. It's been ages.'

'You are the one who has been away,' she said stiffly.

'Yeah, and I want to tell you about it. I thought you might be at *Rainbow* today.'

'I have to look after my brother...'

'That was your brother? I didn't know...'

'You don't need to know!'

'OK. Sorry. Again.'

Tears pooled in her eyes. She didn't want to be playing these silly games. More than anything, she wanted Jason's solid arms around her so that she could bury her head against his chest and cry; tell him what she had been through since she'd seen him last.

'Ro?' His eyes searched her face. 'What's up?' His mouth tightened. 'It's your parents again, isn't it?'

'I really don't want to...' she started.

'It's OK, I get it.' The sun had come out. He tousled his hair and wiped his palms against his jeans. He laced his fingers through hers. 'This OK?'

She nodded.

'Let's go for a walk. There was something I wanted to show you at Thorn Hill, remember?'

Rain sparkled on the grass. There were new swings since she'd last been there with Albi and the climbing frame looked freshly painted.

'Where are we going?'

He led her downhill through a canopy of trees. Roza squealed as a branch shook its water on to their heads.

'Close your eyes. Only another ten steps.'

Roza counted in her head and waited.

'You can look now.'

They were standing in a clearing. Just in front of them stood a raised platform circled by vertical iron bars. The gold paint was worn and weeds had pushed through the cracks in the concrete, but there was a faded elegance about it.

Jason stepped forward and rubbed his hand across a brass plaque.

Thornley Combe Bandstand. Billy Boscoe and his steel band played here on Sunday afternoons: 1960–1967.

Roza turned. Jason's face was a picture of pride like he'd just won a prize.

'My grandad. He was a local celebrity; a pannist. Played the steel drums. He lived with us for a while – me and my mum.'

'So you could look after him?'

'More like the other way round.' Jason's face clouded over. 'My dad died when I was twelve. Mum went to pieces – started drinking, lost her job. Gave herself a stroke in the end. Last year, Grandad died really suddenly. Heart failure, they said.' Jason ground the toe of his trainer into the gravel. 'Life got all messy after that. We tried it for a bit, me and Mum on our own. Then the Social got involved and found this other place for her. Like I couldn't look after her myself.'

'But you were only sixteen . . .'

He growled. 'Then they said I was too young to live on my own.'

'So Wendy gave you a home.'

'Yeah – there are worse places to live. 'Cept when she goes on about my education. Does my head in. You've heard her.'

He picked up a stone and aimed it at the metal pole. It made a clanging noise and bounced off.

'Why did you go away, Jason?'

His face hardened. 'I wanted to take Mum to visit Dad and Grandad's graves. But the care home wrote to me, said I couldn't. That it was too far away and how would we get there?' He looked at Roza. 'Sorry about the way I reacted the other day. I didn't know what to do after that– see Mum or go surfing? Greg's dad owns a flat in Bournemouth. He let me stay there a couple of nights just to get my head straight. Greg and Josh came down to surf later that week.'

Roza felt the colour rise in her cheeks. *That'd teach her. Jumping to conclusions.*

'You still haven't seen your mum then?'

Jason made the growling noise again. 'I don't want to go and see her in a home that stinks of piss and old ladies' perfume. Reminds me too much of how I've let her down.'

'That's not true! You didn't have any choice about it, Jason.'

Roza pulled out the college flyer she'd been carrying around with her and pressed it into his hand. 'You . . . might not want to look at it now but . . .'

He accepted it with a nod and put it in his pocket..

Roza sat on the edge of the bandstand and let her legs dangle. At least Jason could go and visit his mother. She didn't know when she'd ever see Babi and Mami again. She opened her mouth. Her chest was bursting with the effort of keeping it all in.

A breeze blew from somewhere, scattering a pile of dead leaves. Jason hooked his arm around her neck and stroked the side of her face. Slowly she turned her head. There were dashes of yellow in his irises, like little splinters of sunshine. She hadn't been close enough to notice them before.

She held her breath. Any second now he would break the silence, say something funny or turn away.

'Thanks for listening,' he said.

He didn't look like he was going anywhere and the way his eyes were searching hers was a hundred miles away from his jokey face. The kiss was still a surprise though, feather-light and sweet. The tightness in Roza's chest melted away. Her first ever, and with someone she really liked.

She buried her head on his shoulder and closed her eyes. She tried to imagine the people who would have come here on a sunny afternoon like this to listen to Jason's Grandad Billy and his steel band. And for a while the ringing applause shut out all the sadness.

Chapter Twenty-Three

'It is just a long weekend, Jozif.' Adelina slapped the brochure in front of her husband.

At the sink, Roza's hand stopped mid-scrub over the greasy grill pan. The leaflet had been on the table all day. Tall pines, families whizzing about on bikes, riding the rapids. It looked idyllic.

'But the children are only just back from a week with my sister.'

'And me? Have I had a holiday? A few days away *together* will do us all good. The boys will love it.' Adelina pursed her lips. 'And I hear the signal there is weak. With luck, no one will be able to get hold of you.'

She clicked her fingers for Roza to clear the table.

'I am not sure your son deserves a weekend away.' Jozif topped up his glass of raki.

Adelina bristled. She sidled over to the mirror and sucked in her cheeks, tilting her head this way and that. 'You know what Mr Morgan thinks. Skender was influenced by a few naughty boys last year. Now that he is in a different class things will be better,

I am certain of it.' Her eyes flashed at Roza. 'Are you listening in on our conversation, *budalla*?

She picked up the brochure with a defiant look at Jozif. 'I will book it tonight.'

Jason was at the top of the ladder counting out loud. He stopped at ten and held his fingers up.

She slotted a fresh sheet on to her clipboard and waited for Jason to give her the final number. She hadn't seen him for over a week. There had been a bank holiday. And Adelina had been around during the other days buying uniforms ready for the new school year.

But today she had managed to get out. Wendy had closed the cafe and asked her and Jason to help with the annual stock count.

'Eighteen, nineteen. That's the soup mix done.' Jason climbed down, jumping off the last three steps.

'You haven't asked why I was late.'

'You are always late,' Roza teased.

He poked her in the ribs. 'Yeah, but I had a special reason today.' He waggled a letter at her.

Roza stared at the letter heading. **_Marwood College._**

'I'm going to do two A levels, part-time. Start next week.' Jason's face was lit up like a Christmas tree. 'I'll have to get some proer work experience if I want to do paramedic training. But until then I can carry on working here.'

'It sounds amazing,' he went on. 'I met the Sociology teacher at registration today. He runs the Duke of Edinburgh scheme for the college. Look good on my CV for later.' He paused to draw breath. 'It's wild – all happened so quick. Sorry, I'm a bit full of it this morning.'

Roza bit down on her lip. *Just a bit.*

He shifted the ladder to the next row of shelves. 'You OK, Ro? You've gone all quiet. I thought you'd be pleased.'

Wendy was standing in the doorway. She hadn't stopped grinning since they'd started. Now Roza understood why. 'You two ready for a break? Off you go. This sunshine won't last for ever.'

Down the road, they joined the queue inside *Patsy's Pasties*.

'When do you start?' she said, putting on a bright voice. *What was wrong with her? She was the one who'd encouraged him.*

She handed over the money to the girl behind the counter and dropped the paper bag into her backpack.

'The 16th.' Jason looked down the high street. 'Where d'you wanna go? Marwood Green for a change?' He waggled a hand from side to side.

Marwood Green. It was on Skender's way home. 'Thorn Hill,' she said. 'Good exercise.'

At the top, she collapsed on to the grass and rolled up her sleeves. 'That climb never gets any easier.'

'College'll be a lot of work, 'specially the written stuff.' Jason bit into the pasty and groaned with pleasure. 'What about you? No chance your father will change his mind and let you come with me?'

Roza rolled her eyes. *Not again!*

'Hey, that's a nasty bruise.'

Last Saturday. She'd burnt the vegetables. Madam had clouted her on her forearm with the rolling pin. It had hurt so much, she thought it might be broken.

Roza yanked her sleeve down. 'You have pastry round your mouth, Jason.'

'Ro?'

'Oh that. It's nothing. Something set off the smoke alarm and I tripped running to open a window.'

She stood up. It was the same every time. Any reference to life at Ridley Road made her want to close down the chat and leave. Today for some stupid reason it made her want to cry too.

Jason tugged her hand. 'Where you off now? We've only just got here. Anyone'd think you didn't want to spend time with me.'

She dropped back on to the grass. He leaned forward and kissed her. 'That's better.'

She pulled a dandelion head out of the grass, blew on it and watched the seeds float away on the breeze.

The Brakas would be away in two weeks.

She gave him a playful look. 'Where could we go if we had a *whole day*?'

'You serious?' He jerked upright.

She grinned

'Where d'you fancy going then?' he said.

She let out a long breath. 'London. Where else?'

Roza had heard the music from the end of Ridley Road.

She slid back the lock on the garden gate. The noise was coming through Skender's window, along with the smell of weed.

Her glance slid across to Mrs Pam peering through an upstairs window.

Adelina would be home within the hour. Roza didn't need to think about the consequences for herself, as well as Skender.

She slithered through her cell window and headed straight for the stairs.

Skender was on the landing, a spliff between his fingers. 'Hey guys, it's *budalla*,' he slurred. 'Say hello, *budalla*.'

Four boys peered down at her. One of them was the skinny lad with glasses and sticking-out ears, the victim of the shoe scuffle a couple of months before. With a lurch forward he clutched his stomach and moaned.

Roza suddenly remembered Lorik, the first time he'd taken drugs. She raced to the top of the stairs, steered the boy into the bathroom and turned away as he vomited noisily into the toilet bowl.

'Marcus is such a wuss.' Skender started to laugh.

Roza turned on him. 'You idiot! Your mother will be home soon.'

'She's working late. Babi Jozif's picking the brat up after work.'

The sick boy crawled out of the bathroom and slumped on the carpet, his long lashes twitching against his cheeks.

As Skender stared at him, the other boys grabbed their blazers and bags. Pushing their way past, they hurtled down the stairs. Only one of them threw a backward glance.

'Do something!' Skender's voice was cracking.

Roza squatted down beside the boy and rolled him on to his side so he wouldn't choke, but she had no idea what to do next.

She glared at Skender. 'Put that spliff down and get Jozif on the phone.'

'I can't! If he comes home and sees . . .'

'Do it . . . now!'

Roza ran a flannel under the cold tap and clamped it against Marcus's forehead. When he didn't respond she tried a second time, flipping his face with drops of water. His eyes flickered open.

'Get him a drink. Quickly!'

Slowly the boy came round. Roza helped him into a sitting position and waited as he sipped from the cup.

Fifteen, twenty minutes passed. Jozif would be home any minute. Marcus leaned against the banister looking dazed. Roza could hear Skender in his room scrunching up pieces of paper, opening and closing drawers. The smell of air freshener drifted on to the landing.

'I'll leave the window open.' Skender was sounding more confident, his speech almost back to normal. 'What will I tell Babi Jozif? Can we get Marcus out now?'

'Don't you even care whether he's all right?' Roza glared up at him.

The boy struggled to his feet and clung on to the banister. His face was parchment pale and there were streaks of vomit on his blazer. 'I don't want my parents to find out,' he said, his voice wobbling.

'It was that older boy with the red hair, wasn't it? He gave it to you.'

Marcus shot a look at Skender.

'You are stupid boys to take drugs,' said Roza. 'Keep away from that boy. You could die.'

Marcus dragged a hand under his nose.

Skender stood over her, a snide smile on his face. 'You've been out again. Where do you go?'

Roza clambered to her feet and squared her shoulders. She was still taller than him. 'If Jozif finds out about this . . . You know he is still looking for reasons to send you away to school, don't you?'

It was another hour before Jozif arrived home with Albi. Another hold-up at the practice he explained, washing his hands at the sink. Nobody was interested in the details. Roza dished up supper wrapping a slice of pizza into a piece of kitchen paper for later.

'You rang me, Skender.' Jozif glanced at his phone and helped himself to more coleslaw. 'Was there a problem?'

The boy didn't even look up. 'Phone was in my pocket. Must have called you by mistake,' he said.

Chapter Twenty-Four

'THEY'VE LEFT YOU ON your own? How did you get your father to agree to that?' Jason tightened his arm around Roza's shoulder as the bus eased into a bend.

Roza sat forward. She didn't want to miss a single one of the Oxford sights. The colleges, the clocks, the churches. If only she could press the rewind button like you could on TV.

A sign for Christchurch Meadow! Mrs Cicu's husband had been a student at the college.

Ten minutes later they joined the dual carriageway heading for London.

Roza dug Jason in the ribs. '*You* thought you were old enough to live on *your* own.' It hadn't crossed her mind he would consider it odd. 'Where my family come from, children grow up quickly. Not like you British kids – mollycoddled all the time!'

He laughed. He liked that. A new word she had come across.

She had done it again. Wriggled out of a tricky situation with a lie. How practised she had become. After three months, Jason deserved to know who she really was. She sneaked a sideways glance at him. Not now though. She didn't want anything to spoil their day.

'That a new skirt?' The way he was looking at her gave her the shivers.

'I thought you'd never notice. And my sandals.' She wiggled her toes, freshly painted with Adelina's red polish.

The key in her pocket dug into her thigh. Jozif had left it on the kitchen table propped up against the salt cellar. Another one of his *gestures*. Did it really salve his conscience knowing she could go in and out the back door this weekend?

Relax... and breathe.

Jason glanced across at her. He was doing that eyebrow crease thing he did when he thought something wasn't right. 'You OK?'

She cuddled up to him. 'Of course. Why wouldn't I be?'

It was a day she'd never forget. And for all the right reasons... at first.

When they stepped out at Victoria, the sky opened up like a big blue umbrella.

Glossy red buses and taxi cabs queued between traffic lights. Jason pulled her into a shop front to let the crowds pass. He opened up a map on his phone. He studied it for a moment. Then he seized her hand.

'C'mon, let the adventure begin,' he said, seizing her hand. Roza had never seen him so focussed and eager.

Half an hour later they were at the foot of Big Ben. Then it was on to Westminster Bridge. Roza stopped for a moment to look down at the river. A small boy with a mop of blond hair just like Ylli's looked up from a pleasure boat and flapped his Union Jack flag at her. She lifted her hand back and smiled.

Then they were off again. She had no idea where, just that there was a crazy number of people everywhere as though something special was going on. Before she knew it, they were tail-ing a party of Japanese tourists along a familiar wide avenue. Buckingham Palace was straight ahead, with a special flag flying. The queen must be inside. Roza remembered the postcard she'd promised to send Stefanie.

It was wonderful, all of it. If only she could slow the day down.

Outside the palace, Jason said they should give up trying to squeeze through the crowds to the railings. A bus came along and when he'd checked it was going in the right direction he pulled her on board.

'I wanted to watch the guards tripping the colour.' Roza's mouth pulled down at the corners.

Jason chuckled. '*Trooping* the colour.'

They paid the driver and sat down. 'Tell you what. If we've got time, we'll come back this way and you can make faces at the guys wearing the bearskins. Try and make them smile – you'll never do it.'

Roza didn't see what was so funny.

'Hyde Park next.' He checked the map.

'You have a surprise for me there?'

'Yeah. Kind of.' He looked uncertain. 'Not like Buck Pal though. Don't get your hopes up.'

A woman standing next to them in a sari pressed the bell. People were queuing up to get off.

As soon as they crossed the pillared entrance to the park Jason veered off on to a side path.

'Are we looking for something special?' Roza narrowed her eyes. At least it was quieter here – a couple strolling hand in hand, a family of four with a double buggy. She hazarded a guess. 'Another bandstand?'

'Just you wait. This one's a lot posher.'

She couldn't argue with that. Five minutes later they were staring at an octagonal roof shaped like a pagoda, with wrought iron balustrades shining glossy black. No chipped paintwork here or weeds sprouting through the cracks

'Did your grandad's band play here too?'

'Just the once, I think. I came with Mum and Dad when I was seven or eight. Only thing I remember was Grandad Billy lifting me on to his shoulders to wave to the crowd.' Jason looked pensive. 'It was Mum's idea to come. She really loved Grandad. That's why he moved in when Dad died.'

'He sounds like a really special person.'

'Yeah.' Jason grinned. He was remembering something. 'We had a lot of laughs too.'

'Your mother must miss you, Jason.' *Like I miss mine.* 'What do you think your grandad would want you to do for her?'

Jason climbed the steps and pushed his hands into his pockets.

'You could take her out for a walk in her wheelchair if you don't like visiting her indoors. Didn't you say there was a park across the road? That's what Wendy does with her old neighbour.' Roza skipped up the steps after him and gave a nervous laugh. 'Is it OK? To stand up here?'

Jason pulled her towards him by the collar of her jacket. He ran his finger softly down her nose, then kissed her and hugged her tight. She hadn't overdone it then.

'All this talk about food is making me hungry,' he said.

Roza laughed. 'We haven't been talking about food.'

'Well, we should've been.' Jason pulled his phone out. 'It's a half hour walk from here but it'll be worth it.'

'Jason, I don't need any more surprises, this has already been the best day of my life.'

He looped his arm through hers and started walking.

'What?' She giggled. 'Jason, where are you taking me now?'

She was the first one to spot it – the small tables on the pavement, the red flags with double headed eagles either side of a gold awning. *Rozabela's*. Her eyes opened wide. 'An Albanian cafe?' And with *her* name. Well, almost. It was perfect. She spun round. 'Oh my gosh, how did you find it?'

She was now desperate to sit down and rest her throbbing feet. Outside would have been perfect, the pavement still in full sun, but every table was occupied.

Inside, a very young waiter with a round black stud in one ear showed them to the back.

'There's more than you think. Albanian places to eat, I mean.' Jason looked pleased with himself.

Roza ran her finger down the menu. '*Qebapa*! That's what I'll have. It's a sandwich filled with tiny minced-meat patties and cheese. If it's not too expensive?'

'My treat, I told you.'

'I'd like to pay for something.' She twisted her hands, remembering the only other time she'd eaten in a restaurant.

Without thinking she told him about Aunty Sade's 50th birthday. 'It was a really classy place. Babi made a big thing about wanting to pay for the drinks, then found he didn't have enough cash on him. He was so embarrassed. And Aunty didn't let him off the hook easily, crowing about how wealthy she was.'

'Wow.' Jason stopped browsing through the food choices. 'That's the first time you've told me anything about your family. Your aunty sounds like a piece of work.'

Stupid! How had she let that out?

She went back to the menu. 'You should try kofta or a burger, but make sure to ask for plenty of feta to go with it.' If she kept smiling, he wouldn't hear the tremor in her voice.

'You must have food like this all the time at home?' Jason said when they had been served.

Roza fiddled with her napkin. 'Not really.' She took another bite of her sandwich.

'If I was Albanian, I'd never want to eat anything else. This stuff is very good.' Jason's phone beeped. He grinned at the screen. 'Greg says hi.'

'Never mind Greg. Have I told you what a wonderful day I am having?' Roza stretched out her arms. It *was* wonderful. She didn't want thoughts about Aunty Sade spoiling it.

'I think you might have mentioned it once or twice.' He slid his phone towards her. 'OK, Marco Polo. See if you can work out the quickest route back to Buck Pal. And order us a piece of that tu . . . tulumba.' He pointed to the chilled counter and the pieces of fried batter glistening with syrup.

Roza gave up examining the street map as soon as Jason slipped through the candy-striped curtain to the toilet. He obviously didn't know her well enough yet. Her sense of direction was practically non-existent. She glanced around for the waitress to ask for that tulumba.

The cafe was almost empty now. There were a couple of old men having a friendly argument and a dumpy silver-haired woman in the window seat with her head bent into a book. She was wearing a dark mac, even though it was a sunny day. Now she twisted in her seat, flexing her neck. Something in the action seemed familiar but Roza couldn't place her. She waited for her brain to catch up. Was it someone she'd seen at *Rainbow*?

A chunky chain bracelet slid down the woman's arm as she ran a comb through her grey curls. That was enough!

Roza whipped back round. Her breath felt like it was trapped in her throat, her body bolted to the seat. A breeze blew through from the back, lifting the plastic curtain strips.

She kept her head down, her eyes fixed on Jason's phone screen. After a few seconds, she heard a chair scrape and then soft footsteps behind her.

'Well, hello.' There was no mistaking the high, throaty voice.

If she dared to look up, Roza knew Dori's pouchy jowls and pink cheeks would be reflected in the coffee machine.

'I thought it was you when you came in. You nearly slept through the final call at Tirana.' She leaned in close, half-whispering the words as though it was a secret between them.

Roza thought she might throw up. *Look her in the eye. She does not have the power to hurt you – not here, not now.*

The woman straightened, flattened a ten-pound note next to the till. 'What a surprise,' she said sweetly, clasping her hands in front of her. 'Does your cousin know you've come to London?'

Roza gripped the edge of the table and hauled herself to her feet. She had a question of her own. What had happened to the two girls travelling with her?

But the words stuck in her throat like a sweet, swallowed whole.

Dori shut her bag with a snap and hooked it over her arm. 'Well, goodbye . . . I have quite forgotten your name.'

'Everything OK, Roza?' At last, Jason was there.

'Roza. Of course.'

Chapter Twenty-Five

Roza pushed past him. She just made it to the toilet.

When she'd finished throwing up, she tried to stand. It felt like someone drumming in her head. She wiped her mouth with a handful of tissues and leaned against the cubicle door.

Jason was waiting for her outside. 'What was *that* about? Who was that woman?'

He steered her across the road to a stretch of grass with a war memorial at the far end.

Roza dropped on to the first bench they came to and let her head fall forward. All she wanted to do was stay there, not say anything, wait for Jason to work it out on his own. But he wasn't going to. She pressed her fists into her eye sockets. She would have to put it into words. Then what? Would he think differently about her? Understand why she hadn't told him?

He sat beside her. 'That's how you looked in the lane when I first saw you, with your hair all over your face, your fists balled up. Tell me, Ro, what's going on?'

By the time she had finished, long, lacy shadows were dancing across the grass. Roza's hands weren't shaking any more. She felt lighter. It was a relief to have finally shared her secret. She peered up into Jason's face. He hadn't moved the whole time she'd been speaking – his elbows digging into his knees, his eyes fixed on some point in the distance.

He straightened up. 'So, let me get this straight. Your family *arranged* this . . .?'

'Albania has one of the worst records for trafficking people to Britain,' Roza said. 'And doing it through the extended family, is not unusual apparently.'

Jason tapped the side of his head. 'There was something in the news last year – Vietnamese people dying of suffocation in a lorry trailer.' He grimaced. 'I had no idea kids were caught up in it as well.'

'Those bruises. They were from her, weren't they?' He made a noise like a dog snarling. 'I'm an idiot. I should have guessed.' His gaze moved up to her face. 'What I don't understand is . . .'

Here it comes. The question she'd been dreading.

'Why didn't I tell you?' She bit down on her lip focussing on the patch of ground between her feet. 'I think because . . . I was ashamed that this terrible thing had happened to me. Why would I tell you what my life was really like? I wanted to keep my life away from the Brakas separate. You and Wendy, working in *Rainbow* – it's what has kept me going.'

Jason nodded. He seemed to understand. 'And that old biddy in the cafe – you think she's in on it too?'

'I saw her at the airport before Aunty told me we were travelling together. I thought she was just another passenger; a grandmother travelling with a baby and an older girl. Not someone who would do bad things. But in the rest room, changing the baby's nappy . . .' Roza shuddered. 'When the baby kicked her, she lashed out – shook the child and slapped her really hard. Not like a relative or someone who cared. I got out as fast as I could. Then Aunty told me somebody called Dori would see me on to the plane. Next thing I knew, the woman in the toilet was pinching my shoulder to wake me. Our flight had been called.'

Roza twisted round and locked eyes with Jason. 'She might look like a sweet old lady but she's a courier, I'm convinced of it. Bringing the two girls to the UK to be sold.'

Jason tousled his hands through his hair. With a rush of air, he stood up.

'You *have* to go to the police, Ro. You've got no choice.'

'And risk being returned to the Brakas? Are you serious? I have told you what happened before.'

'That doesn't mean it would happen again. Anyway, it's not just about you now, is it? All those other kids are involved.'

Roza jumped up. 'Do you think I don't know that?'

'So you're gonna do *nothing*?' Jason threw his hands up. 'There must be people who'll help you. *I* want to help you!'

'Well, you can't, and you mustn't tell anyone. No one, do you hear me? Even if the police *did* believe my story this time, I still wouldn't feel safe. They would put me in a hostel and people like Adelina and Dori would come looking for me. Children taken into care go missing all the time. Most of them back into the hands of the people who trafficked them.'

'Then tell the police you want to go back to Albania.'

'Jason, you have no idea.' Her insides felt like they were folding up. She dropped back on to the bench. 'Why are you so angry with me? This is not my fault.'

Jason was still on his feet. 'I don't understand. Why d'you have to be so *stubborn*? So . . . so *independent*?' He was shouting now.

'Hey, mate.' A man was marching up to them, trailing two small boys. One of them was carrying a football. The man stepped up close to Jason. 'Keep a lid on it, will ya? This is a kiddies' play area.'

'Sorry.' Jason coloured up, looked down.

'C'mon boys.' The man led them away.

Jason pulled the zip up on his jacket. 'I'll wait for you by the road,' he mumbled.

Roza watched him walk away, his shoulders slouched.
So this is what happens next. Now she knew.

They walked back to the bus station in silence, separated by a gap a metre wide. No one would have guessed they were even together.

When the bus pulled up at the end of Ridley Road, Jason made a sudden grab for her hand. 'Don't go back there, Ro. You can stay with us. I'll talk to Wendy.'

Roza shook him off and glared. 'You don't tell Wendy anything, Jason. I mean it.'

The house was hot and airless. Roza left the back door open. With the windows locked it was all she could do.

Tea, she needed tea. She switched on the kettle, thinking of the half-finished cup in *Rozabela's* and the tulumba they'd never got to order.

How had Jason morphed from being her dream date to someone she hardly recognised? Accusing her of not doing anything then giving her the silent treatment all the way back to Thornley. She couldn't work it out. Unless . . . unless it was to do with his mother. His frustration at not being able to help her boiling over so now he was trying to help *Roza* instead.

She let the idea percolate with her cup of tea.

The more she thought about it, it was the only explanation that made any sense. He wanted to be her hero. Sort out her life for her. Well, she didn't need him to do that thank you very much! In a couple of weeks she'd have her four hundred pounds. Enough to leave Thornley for good – do things her own way, find Mr Monet. Out of Jason's life for good too – this *stubborn, independent* girl.

She went into the lounge and turned on the TV – an American romcom was playing... The couple at the drive-in were closing in for a kiss.

Jason's hands tugging the collar of her jacket, his lips featherlight and soft. She stabbed the red button and tossed the remote across the sofa.

A sudden gust blew the lounge door open. It was then she saw the light on the hall phone.

Slowly Roza got up and walked towards it. She pressed the play button. Dori's high voice was cold and hard now..

What was your girl doing in London on Saturday? Your carelessness is putting the whole operation at risk. If it happens again, she will have to be moved to a different location.

A different location. Almost the same words Jozif had used.

With trembling fingers, Roza pressed replay and listened for the electronic voice. She pushed the key and waited.

Message erased.

She was safe. But for how long?

Chapter Twenty-Six

Roza stretched out on the grass and flexed her toes. She closed her eyes and tipped her head back, letting the sun soak into her skin. Simple pleasures like these would soon be a memory. The Brakas were back tomorrow.

'Oh, it's you.' Mrs Pam was giving her the once-over from the other side of the fence, taking in the long scruffy t-shirt she wore to sleep in

Roza sat up with a start. She wanted to run inside but then Mrs Pam would see how it only came down to the tops of her legs.

'I was just saying to Mrs Henderson next door how quiet it's been without all the usual racket. Left you behind, have they?'

Roza felt like saying something rude in return.

The doorbell chimed.

She stretched her t-shirt down as far as it would go, scrambled to her feet and ran to peek between the lounge curtains

Jason was on the doorstep peering through the letterbox and clutching a bunch of yellow roses. Roza's body sagged with relief until she remembered how upset she still was with him.

She pulled on yesterday's skirt and top and scurried round to the front of the house. When she saw Jason he pulled her against his chest. She hadn't intended to let him do that.

She scowled at him. 'How did you find out where I live?'

'Last night, I got off at the next stop. Ran back and watched you go up the lane.'

'So you have stopped being cross with me now?'

'I just wanna help you, Ro. The thought of you living here with these ... these *scumbags*.'

Roza marched back along the lane and let him follow. Something else for Mrs Pam to gossip about.

Jason propped his bike against the back wall. His face was shiny with sweat. 'Can I get a glass of water?'

Roza watched as he drank it down in one go. Clearly he had something to say. It made her feel on edge. She didn't have the energy for another row.

He rubbed his forehead with the back of his hand. 'I had another reason for coming. No, two. Wendy's cooking a roast. She said to invite you.'

'You have not told her?'

His hands shot up. 'I wouldn't dare!'

'Wendy has never invited me to her house before.'

'She knew you were on your own today.'

'Jason?'

'She *has* asked me about your family – if I've met them, what they're like? Not today, but on and off. She worries about you; thinks you don't eat properly, says it's not normal that you never talk about them.'

'And what did you say?'

'I told her what I used to think. That your father's strict, thinks girls shouldn't stay on at school, doesn't like you seeing boys.'

She thought for a moment. 'OK. Lunch would be nice. Wendy is very kind.'

'This is the other reason I came.' Jason reached into his back pocket and pressed a mobile phone into her palm. He closed her fingers around it. 'It's an old one of Wendy's. Pay-as-you-go.'

It didn't look old; pink and sparkly.

'I got you a new cover. The old one was a bit basic.'

He spent the next twenty minutes showing her how to send text messages, make calls and charge the battery.

'I've given you a special ringtone, so you'll know when it's me calling. Listen.'

Roza let the weird tune play for a few seconds. 'It sounds like somebody singing under water.'

'It's called *Blue Whale*. Promise you'll use it to call me if you're in trouble.'

She folded her arms. 'And how will you rescue me, Jason? Break the door down?'

He brought his face up so close she could have counted his freckles. 'Promise me!'

'OK, OK, I promise.'

She went upstairs to pull on her jeans and a clean top. She could hear his trainers squeaking as he moved about the hall, gently opening and closing doors. She tensed at the thought he might find her cell and perhaps carry on like he had yesterday, insisting she go to the police.

When she came down to look for him he was lying on the grass, screening his face from the sun.

'Ready?' he said.

Wendy was juggling steaming saucepans when they arrived. Jason presented her with the roses. 'From both of us,' he said, with a wink at Roza.

Roza felt suddenly shy. It was different from being at the café. She knew what she was doing there.

'I like the pattern on your blouse,' she said to Wendy. She looked younger today, more like an older sister than an aunt.

While Jason laid the table, Wendy asked Roza if she would chop parsley for a sauce to go with the ham.

'So how was your trip to London?' Wendy's eyes twinkled. She was looking for a more colourful answer than a list of the places they had visited.

Roza's cheeks flushed.

'It may be hard to believe lovey, but I was young once.'

Wendy drained one of the saucepans into the sink. Her voice dropped to a whisper. 'He's very fond of you, y'know. Not that he'd say anything to me, of course. And it's good he's going to college, isn't it? I know you'll encourage him to stick at it.'

Lunch went much better than Roza expected. She watched Wendy's eyes as she described how much Jason was like his father; his *winning ways* always getting him out of trouble.

Could she be any different from Aunty Sade?

The food turned sour in Roza's mouth. Quietly she put her knife and fork down.

'Too much for you, lovey?' asked Wendy. 'Or saving yourself for pudding?'

Jason tickled the back of Roza's neck as they followed Wendy into the kitchen. 'You OK?'

His phone buzzed and he moved to the back door to answer it.

'I thought you would have a dishwasher?' Roza said, picking up a tea towel.

Wendy tittered. 'Don't need one – not when Jason's around. Washes up most evenings for me, don't you sweetheart?'

But Jason was sauntering across the grass, his phone clamped against his ear.

While Wendy carried on talking, Roza dried a soapy glass and watched him. It didn't look like a light-hearted conversation with one of his friends.

'. . . so it would be a *big* help if you could cover her shift this Thursday.'

'Sorry?' Roza spun round.

'Carla. She's driving her daughter up to an open day in Birmingham.'

'You want me to serve at the tables?'

'Just the one shift. You've seen what she does. You could start waitressing regularly after that, if you like. I could pay you a bit more that way.'

Wendy took the tea towel from Roza. 'Head in the clouds today. You go out and join his lordship.' She clicked her tongue. 'Now he's off his phone. The rest of these will dry by themselves in this heat.'

Jason walked towards her with a smile that looked like it was pasted on.

'Is everything all right?' Roza said. 'That was a long call.'

He led her to the cushioned seat at the end of the garden. Roza sat down and fanned herself with her hand.

'Just a mate at college. About a project we're working on.'

'Really?'

His face tensed.

'No! Listen to me, Ro. I've worked out how you can get away from Ridley Road without having to go to the police.'

'Oh Jason! Not this again!'

'Just hear me out, OK? This teacher on my course, Jim Rogers, the one I told you about who runs the D of E? I found out he used to be a social worker, so he knows how the system works.'

'That was who you were talking to?'

'Yeah'. He was smiling properly now, thinking he had done her a huge favour. 'He'll help us if he can. He's said so.'

He began to explain about going to a *place of safety*, probably a foster home. 'Only for a bit though. Till they sort out how you came here in the first place.'

'You *told* him, after I asked you to keep it to yourself? I trusted you, Jason.' She stood up and backed away. 'And what do you mean help *us*? This has happened to *me*, not you. I have already told you – I do not want that kind of help.'

Jason shook his head. 'What other kind d'you think there is?'

She blew out several short breaths. 'There is a man in London. A journalist. Before I left Albania my teacher gave me a card with his name and address. She told me he was a good man and if ever I was in trouble, he would help me.'

'And?'

'I have not been able to find him, not yet.'

'You said you had his address.'

She was getting flustered. 'I . . . I lost the card. No, the truth is I threw it away and . . . that was a very foolish thing to do.'

Jason screwed up his face. She was making no sense at all. Going back to the beginning she tried to explain. How Jason's *Sunrise* painting had triggered the memory of the man's name. About searching for him on the internet. By the time she had finished, Jason was staring at her open-mouthed as if she had turned into some kind of crazy-girl.

'That's it?' He rubbed the back of his neck as though he had no idea what to say next. Then his voice became slow and deliberate as though he was explaining something very simple to a small child.

'How d'you think you're gonna find this person? He could be living anywhere. And even if he *is* in the UK and you *do* track him down, you don't know for sure he'll help you. Look, Jim says there's nothing for you to be afraid of. He's a great guy. Won't you just agree to meet him?'

Any minute, her heart was going to explode. Him and his Mr Jim, talking about her as if she were a project; a problem to be solved. Roza took a deep breath. She had to stay calm.

'You are not listening to me, Jason. I have already told you; I don't want to talk to social workers or the police or anyone. You have no idea what is best for me. Now sort out your own troubles and stop meddling in mine.'

'*My* troubles?'

'Your mother, Jason. You think you have let her down since your grandfather died. That if you can do something to help *me*, be *my* hero, that will make you feel better. But it won't! You have to go and make things right with your mother. Visit her. Talk to her. But please . . . Leave. Me. Alone!'

Without another word, Jason sprang up and rushed past Wendy, who had come out to see what was going on. A few moments later, the door slammed.

Chapter Twenty-Seven

ADELINA WAS CONDUCTING A tour of the downstairs rooms – rearranging ornaments, straightening the pile of magazines, pulling the curtains into tidier folds. Roza stood as usual on the kitchen doormat and chewed her lip. There were no clues for Madam to pick up. No bus tickets or receipts, no trace of Jason having been there. Most important of all, the light on the phone was not flashing. Dori had not called back.

'Everything appears to be in order.' Adelina came into the kitchen. She planted herself in front of the mirror teasing the spiky ends of her fringe into place. 'Tomorrow you will move Albi's things in with Skender. The decorator is coming on Friday.' She swivelled around. 'Now, get my baby ready for bed.'

Poor little Albi. Moving in with his bully brother. Roza would have to keep a close eye.

Skender was in his room. His eyes didn't move, as Roza passed with Albi, as if they were actually glued to his phone. Were those tears rolling down his cheeks? Roza's chest tightened. If things weren't right for Skender they usually ended up being bad for her.

She hardly slept that night. The harsh words volleyed between her and Jason replayed in her head. *Sort out your own troubles... stop meddling in mine... it's not just about you.*

The next morning her anger still clung to her like a second skin. Didn't he understand? Hadn't he been listening at all? She needed to follow her own plan. Track down Mr Monet, find her way back to Babi so she could hear him say he never meant these awful things to happen to her. If she couldn't do that, nothing would be right. Ever.

It had taken her months to trust anyone. Now the person she'd chosen had betrayed her. It was over between her and Jason.

Time for her to leave. What was she waiting for? To wake up and find a neon sign painted on the back lawn? She studied her reflection in Albi's mirror. So what if she was still seventy pounds short of her target? She must be positive. With her experience in *Rainbow* she was sure to find a job in a cafe or hotel.

Thursday. She'd cover Carla's shift like she'd promised Wendy, then catch the coach to London.

The next morning, Roza went to the library. Clearing Albi's room could wait.

There were plenty of websites advertising cheap places to stay in London. She printed off details of the *Hamlet Hostel*. It looked a bit run-down but it was cheaper than the rest and only a ten-minute walk from Victoria. It would do until she could get a job and find somewhere to rent.

She sat back and stared out of the window. A boy in a beanie ran past and for a second she thought it was Jason. Leaving without setting things right between them felt wrong, but she couldn't face going round to Wendy's and having another row. She fiddled with her pen, clicking it on and off. She could write him a letter. Tell him she was leaving for London to carry on with her search for Mr Monet. Apologising for the things she'd said was a step too far, but she could say sorry for the way things had ended, that she hoped his mother would get better soon and they'd make up. *Yes!* She'd leave the note with Wendy. It was better than nothing.

Roza's eyes flicked back to the blank computer screen. Just the other small matter of finding Mr Monet then. Her fingers hovered over the keyboard. She didn't have to wait till she got to London.

'What are you working on today?' Mr Joe appeared behind her with the trolley, slotting books back on to the shelves.

Roza folded her pages of printing and stuffed them into her backpack. 'I'm trying to find someone,' she said lightly. 'A family friend in London. His name is Monet, like the painter. At least I think it is.'

'Maybe I can help. My sister-in-law roped me in to research her family tree last year.' He dragged a seat across.

'I don't know for sure but I think he writes about human rights stuff,' Roza made space next to her. She couldn't bring herself to use the words *people trafficking*.

'OK. Well, Monet *is* an unusual name. Have you tried similar names or different spellings? *Menet. Manet. Monnay?*' He spelled them all out as he typed.

Roza leaned forward. Nothing new on the screen so far.

'Add another "t" to Monet.' She hesitated. 'And an "e" on the end.'

She didn't know what made her say it but the letters looked right somehow. As if she'd seen them before.

'Did you say he was a journalist?' Mr Joe sat back and pointed to the screen. 'Think that might be him?'

Michael Monette. b. 1976. British journalist . . . His recent investigations into forced labour and slavery . . .

Roza read the line again. *Michael Monette.* A photograph appeared. A long narrow face, dark-framed glasses, a forehead puckered with worry lines.

She followed the script down the page.

... have led to a ban on visiting these countries. Working freelance and based in North London, Monette has been prolific in exposing ...

A woman at the desk called Mr Joe's name.

Roza carried on scrolling and opening links. *Click, click.* More photos of the man appeared between paragraphs of text. One showed him in a light linen jacket shaking hands with a man in military uniform. In another he was part of a group posing for a photo in front of an official-looking building. Roza thought she recognised it from the civic centre in Tirana. Next to him, a woman dressed in traditional Albanian clothes was laughing. Her hair coiled into a bun, her hand resting lightly on his shoulder.

Roza double-clicked on the image. A small choking sound escaped from the back of her throat. It was Mrs Cicu!

She glanced at the clock. She needed to get back to Ridley Road.

'Come back tomorrow if you need any more help,' called Mr Joe.

Roza nodded, too excited to speak. She could have hugged him.

It didn't matter any more, not reaching her target. Now she knew where Michael Monette lived, she could travel to North London and find him. He would help her find her way home.

24 September. 18.25 pm

Text message from Sade to Adelina

I have some bad news. Call me tonight 9 p.m. Albanian time. Use this burner phone. The police are looking for me. Roza's teacher has been stirring things up.

Chapter Twenty-Eight

THE NEXT MORNING ADELINA announced Skender was ill.

'I am sure he has a fever. He was sick in the night.'

Jozif's lips tightened as he slathered butter over his toast. 'Something to do with the missed calls I picked up from the school?' He held out his phone. 'Two. While we were away.'

'If it is anything important, they will call again,' Adelina said briskly. Her eyes flashed at Roza. 'Don't disturb him. He is sleeping.'

When the other three had left, Roza tiptoed up the stairs. She had been intending to have a final look for her passport in Jozif's study. She could hardly do that now. Skender's door was partly open, the bathroom door locked. Perhaps he *did* have an upset stomach.

A muffled twanging noise drew her eye to his bed. She lifted the duvet and flipped his phone over. A message from his friend Manny.

Mate the stories been goin round Mog knows bout that party your dad's gonna find out.

It needed a bit of thinking about – and a few full stops – but she got the gist.

More than two weeks had passed since she'd caught Skender and his friends taking drugs. Now someone had told the head teacher – *the Mog*. Skender used that nickname for him a lot.

The toilet flushed. The tap gushed. Tossing the phone back on the bed she flew down the stairs.

She didn't need a crystal ball to tell her what would happen next. Skender would be on the next train to boarding school. And he wouldn't think twice about spilling *her* secrets. Waiting until Thursday to leave Thornley was out of the question now. She had to get away . . . today!

Her fingers wouldn't work fast enough. Stuffing spare clothes into her bag, making sure the information she'd printed off at the library was there too. And the rest of her money. She mustn't forget that. Stretching over the washing machine she unhooked the plastic pouch from the back.

Footsteps thundered down the stairs. There was no time to hide the pouch in her backpack. Her coat hanging on the back of her cell door would have to do. Where she'd already put the note for Jason.

As she dropped the bundle of notes into one of the big patch pockets her cell door flew open and hit the wall with a bang. 'Was it you, *budalla*? Snitching on me to the school?'

Roza pushed both hands into his chest. 'Don't be so stupid. Why would I do that? One of your friends must have told their parents.'

The boy narrowed his eyes as though he was working it out. He nodded. 'Yeah. Bet it was Marcus,' he said with a snort. 'Proper mummy's boy. He probably had nightmares.'

His phone trilled. 'Manny!'

He grabbed a handful of biscuits from the tin on the counter and headed for the stairs. 'What we gonna do, Man? Don't tell me not to panic. My step-dad – he's gonna send me away, I know he is.'

Skender's door closed.

Roza grabbed her backpack, heart racing. The next bus to Oxford left in forty minutes. There was just one thing she needed to do first.

'I wasn't expecting you today, lovey. Everything all right?' Wendy came to the door of the cafe, wiping her hands on her apron.

It all spilled out in a breathless monologue, the story Roza had been concocting on the way. About her grandmother. Gjyshe wasn't well (that part at least was true). She had to go and stay with her in London for a couple of weeks. Roza took in a gulp of air.

Wendy's eyes travelled down to the carrier bag of clothes between her feet. 'Off right away then, are you?' She raised an eyebrow.

'Someone will meet me at Victoria.' Roza fixed her eyes on a spot over Wendy's shoulder. She had never been any good at telling untruths.

'Do you want me to tell Jason? He's not here or I'd ...'

'Would you give him this?'

Roza reached for the letter and froze. Her coat! It had been so warm all week she hadn't even thought to put it on. Now fat drops of rain had started, landing like full stops on the pavement.

'You all right, lovey?'

What time is it? I can't leave without my coat.

She must have said the words out loud because when she looked into Wendy's face, expecting her to say, Now tell me what's really going on, all she said was, Ten to two.

The London coach ran every hour, didn't it? She'd just have to catch the next one.

Roza didn't see her until she had slithered through the window and on to the couch. Adelina. They were eyeball to eyeball.

The woman pushed her roughly against the wall. 'I come home early to deal with accusations against my son and what do I find?' She waved the bundle of money – Roza's money – in her face. 'Skender says he found it in here, in your coat pocket. Where did you steal it from you little tramp?'

Skender sidled into view behind his mother, a fresh red weal on his cheek.

'I have been working.' Roza spat the words out. She wanted Adelina to know that she had not succeeded in keeping her a prisoner. 'That money is what *I* have earned. *And* I have been studying at the library. Going out every day in fact.'

'You little . . .' Adelina hauled her into the kitchen by her sleeve. Roza's head hit the wall and the next moment she was on the floor, a taste of blood in her mouth. Lights sparked in front of her eyes.

'Adelina! Enough!'

Jozif. Thank God.

His voice was weary. 'The girl is still here. She has not tried to make trouble.'

'You fool! You don't know that.' Adelina wiped a gob of spittle from her lips. 'We could have a pair of do-gooders from the council on our doorstep at any moment.' She pointed to the cell window. 'Why has she been able to get out? It should be screwed down like the others.'

Jozif made a pretence of examining it. 'A rusty lock appears to be the problem. I will repair it immediately.'

'And what do we have in *here*?' Adelina pounced on Roza's backpack which had fallen to the floor. She shook the contents on to the kitchen table.

'Planning to leave us, were you?' She held up the sheets Roza had printed off. 'You think there is anything for you to go back to?' A mean smile played around her lips.

Roza cradled her head. Her fingers were sticky with blood, her head throbbing. 'My father . . . still cares about me. He will understand . . . what really happened . . . that your mother lied and tricked him . . . and that you . . .'

'I don't think so. You won't be hearing from *him* again.'

There was a look of triumph on Adelina's face. Her lips twitched. 'There was a car crash last week. Your family are all dead.'

25th September 8.47 p.m: phone call

Sade Adelina? What is it? We spoke only yesterday.

Adelina She cannot remain here any longer.

Sade Roza? (Sade sighs.) I know she was pestering her father to return home and I made it quite clear to him that could not happen.

Adelina She has ... been getting out of the house. It came to light yesterday.

Sade Then lock her in!

Adelina Do you think I haven't done that already?

Sade This situation is of your making, Adelina. None of this would have happened if you had treated her reasonably, as I intended. Sending her to school, a few light chores.

Adelina I told you I would do with her as I pleased. Once she was in my home it was none of your business. Promising her opportunities you denied me! You and that brother of yours.

Sade It was an accident, Adelina. How many times do I have to tell you. Arben was not to blame. (Heavy sigh). Dori told me she saw Roza in London last week, did you know that? If Roza has been making trouble, reporting to others how you have treated her, we need to act with urgency. I will arrange for her to be transferred.

Adelina You mean ...

Sade You've left us with no choice. I will get Dori to contact you and arrange a handover.

Adelina Tell her I expect to be paid for the little witch.

Sade Do I get a thank you, Adelina?

(Phone slammed down.)

Chapter Twenty-Nine

ADELINA'S WORDS SWIRLED AROUND Roza's head. The woman was lying – she had to be – looking for a way to break her spirit. It was a last desperate ploy to crush any hope that Roza might see her family again.

She sagged against her cell door, plucking hopelessly at the cords Jozif had used to bind her wrists. The knock to her head was making everything fuzzy. She had given up trying to make sense of the words firing back and forth between Adelina and Jozif. All she wanted to do was sleep.

She tipped sideways on to the couch. Something hard was digging into her thigh. Jason's phone. She'd charged it up only that morning. *Promise you'll call me if you're in trouble.* Fired with sudden hope, Roza eased it out. She'd have to keep the message short. Her eyesight was blurry, her fingers fat and clumsy on the keys and there was barely any light to see.

At last, the tiny envelope flew off the screen. *Message sent.* This nightmare would soon be over. Jason would not let her down. She let her head flop back and gave into the urge to shut her eyes. Not for long though. Jason and the police would be here soon.

***

Roza knew it was morning. Albi was whining in the kitchen. She should be there too, coaxing him to eat his porridge. Any second now Adelina would charge in and yell at her for oversleeping.

She fumbled for her phone.

Help! Locked up. Bring police.

Were those really her words? Twelve hours later they looked silly and melodramatic, like someone playing a joke. Where was Jason? Why hadn't he come?

A key scratched in the lock. In the gap that opened up a square tub appeared. Water splattered over the side. A crust of bread followed, skidding across the floor together with a blue plastic bowl Jozif used to wash the car.

'Please,' Roza cried out. The door closed over. Then the shouts of both boys from the hall followed by the front door shutting.

She tipped forward, lapping at the water like a dog. The crust was hard but edible and she stuffed it into her mouth.

She needed a pee too but that would have to wait.

Another loud bang from the hall made her jump.

Footsteps charged through the kitchen. Her cell door flew open wide.

'Get up! Get up!'

Roza barely recognised Jozif. A mad man with bulging eyes, streaming with sweat and wielding a knife. She whimpered and shuffled backwards, pressing her backbone hard against the wall.

'I have not come to harm you.' He grabbed her wrists and yanked her to her feet. The knife sliced through the cords. 'A man is coming for you. He rang Adelina to arrange it before she left. You must get away.'

Roza stared at him as if through a fog. He might as well have been speaking Japanese.

'Don't you understand?' He was bawling at her now, like she was deaf or stupid. Or both. 'I warned you this would happen. You should have escaped when you had the chance.' He pressed an envelope into her palm. 'This will get you to London. It is easy to get lost there. I will drive you to the station.'

Roza tore the flap. A bundle of notes and her passport. She looked at him. 'I searched everywhere for it.'

'She carried it around with her.' He pulled open the dirty cupboard door. 'This is yours too?'

Her backpack! And – her fingers found their way to the secret pocket – yes, the rest of her money, still there.

Jozif's car was on the drive. He gestured for Roza to get behind the passenger seat. As she squashed herself into the footwell, she heard the whine of the Friday bin lorry from the park end of the road. She raised her head slightly. A vehicle was approaching from the other end too, a dark grey beast that came to a stop two doors down.

Frantically, Jozif manoeuvred backwards and forwards. But their exit was blocked in both directions.

The driver of the 4x4 got out and plodded up the road, ignoring the protests of the lorry driver. Solid with a huge belly and shoulders like a rugby player, his eyes darted between the Braka's house and the scrap of paper his hand.

Suddenly there was a loud smack on the trunk of Jozif's car. Roza yelped. Any second now the man would see her in the back. Had Jozif locked the door?

The dustbin lorry edged forward until it was nose to nose with the 4x4. A gap had opened up.

'Hold tight.' Jozif swung the car sharply to the right and sped down the road with a roar.

Cautiously Roza peered over the back seat.

'Get down for God's sake!' Jozif barked. 'He's on our tail.'

And he was. Following so close that the next time Jozif braked, Roza was certain he would slam into the rear and snatch her from the back.

Shops and houses sped by, as though the fast-forward button was jammed on an action movie. A police siren crescendoed and faded. When at last Jozif screeched to a halt at the bus station in Oxford, the car chasing them was nowhere to be seen. A bus was sitting in the parking bay, its engine purring.

Roza pulled herself up on to the back seat. 'What happened?' she squeaked.

'He ran a red light. The police stopped him. Now, get on the bus and do not come back.'

There was no *Goodbye, godspeed,* even though she was sure that of all the people who had ever travelled from Oxford to London she was the one who would need it the most. Roza straightened her backpack and climbed out of the car.

Chapter Thirty

AT VICTORIA, THE DEPARTURES area was a sea of red and white. There must be a big football match on somewhere. Pushing through to the exit, Roza's legs turned to jelly and lights flickered around her eyes. She dropped on to one of the hard seats with a bump.

'Are you a'right, dear?' A brown-faced woman in a bright orange dress leaning over a luggage trolley frowned at her with concern. She patted Roza's arm and held out a crumpled ten-pound note. 'You can get something to eat over there.' The woman pointed to a food kiosk by the exit.

'No, no, it's fine but thank you.' Roza managed a weak smile. Money was one thing she did have.

She bought a cheese roll and a bottle of water and ate as she walked. Twenty minutes later she was facing a three-storey hostel – *The Dubrovnik*. The white letters were barely large enough to read from the pavement.

Staying at the *Hamlet*, as she had planned, would have been far too risky. Adelina had seen the name. This place looked anonymous enough with its beige-coloured door and steel-framed windows. Roza delved into her bag. Would this place match the nineteen pounds a night rate of the *Hamlet*?

'Only if you share,' came the response when Roza asked. The woman behind the desk had a pale, pinched face under a black headscarf. Seeing Roza falter she added, 'There is another girl on her own. She is away tonight, returning tomorrow. I could put you in with her?'

The room was on the first floor, midway along a corridor with cracked linoleum and strip lighting. A miniature bear had been propped up against the pillow of one bed. Damp t-shirts were draped over the frame. They gave out a pleasant smell but the windows had misted over.

'There's a laundry and a dryer in the basement.'

'Yes, Miss.' Roza didn't want her thinking she was going to be any trouble.

The woman narrowed her eyes. 'You've not done this before, have you?

Well, these are the rules.' She rapped the back of the door with her knuckles.

Roza resisted the temptation to smile. *No problem, I am used to following rules.*

Tiredness settled on her like a great weight after that. She lay on top of the stiff blue cover and fell asleep thinking how strange it would be to sleep in a proper bed at last, even one as lumpy as this.

By the time she woke it was after four.

She had to make a plan! If she could find Mr Monette quickly and he was willing to help her return to Albania, she wouldn't need to look for a job. But if it turned out to be harder than she hoped . . .

Roza counted her money. It looked a lot, but now she was in London she had a better idea how much things cost. Two weeks, three at the most, and it would all be gone.

She pulled her coat on and went outside. Daylight was dwindling, the street and shop fronts all lit up. Pulling up her hood Roza retraced her steps to the tube station she had passed on the way.

Mr Monette lived in North London. That was all she knew. Tracing the Northern Line on the underground map – its black tentacles spreading out like a huge spider's web – the size of the place hit her. *Belsize Park, Kentish Town, North Finchley* – he could be living in any of these places. Or none of them. She could hardly wander the streets knocking on doors. She'd have to think again.

On the way back to the hostel, Roza passed an old church. The front half was covered with scaffolding but the notice board, with its praying hands image and a smiley face emoji, said *Open for Silent Prayer*.

She settled down on one of the cushioned seats at the back and bowed her head. There was a lot to pray about.

Staying safe.
Finding Mr Monette's address quickly.
Looking for a job if that didn't work out.

She took a deep breath, trusting God to see the capital letters in her head as she added her final request. It was the most important one, after all.

FIND OUT WHAT HAS HAPPENED TO MY FAMILY.

She let the silence gather around her. Had they *really* been killed in an accident? She recalled the look of pure spite on Adelina's face. She would have given her more details if it was true. And enjoyed doing that. No, the more Roza thought about it, the more convinced she was that Adelina had made it up. But it felt like a low blow, even for her.

Rain was falling steadily when Roza opened the creaky door and stepped on to the pavement. Cars and buses swished along the wet road. She picked up a bag of chips and a fishcake from a street seller. Remembering *The Dubrovnik*'s rules, she stood under the awning at the hostel's entrance to eat.

The woman at reception earlier was on the phone when Roza headed for the stairs. She covered the handset and beckoned her over.

'A man came here while you were out. Big.' She gestured with her hands; her eyes wide. 'He described you and gave your first name. Were you expecting anyone?'

Roza's legs buckled. Gripping the edge of the desk she shook her head.

'I thought so. I told him there was no one matching that description here and he went away. I didn't like the look of him.'

Roza muttered her thanks and went upstairs.

The man with the big belly was still on her trail. If he was checking each hostel in Victoria, she could have run into him.

She turned the key in the door, only wishing it had a bolt as well. A sudden burst of anger flared inside her.

It was all Jason's fault she was here paralysed by fear. Making Roza promise to text him if she was in trouble; then not coming to her aid. *Idiot!* Why had she ever thought she could trust him?

She pulled out her phone and keyed in his number. It went straight to voicemail.

Angrily, she tapped out a message. *I've figured it out. He's Michael Monette, not Monet, and he lives in North London.* She added *the man my teacher said would help me*, in case Jason had forgotten. And he probably had! Going on and on at her instead of listening to what she had to say.

I'm going to find him, she finished. *So I am doing something, Jason White. Just not what you think I should do!*

Despite everything, Roza slept. She woke with a fresh idea. She'd go to the local library – she'd spotted it near the coach station – and read everything she could find on Michael Monette.

She dressed quickly. It was already after eight. The overnight rain had blown away and the morning was clear and cloudless. It felt like a good sign. She picked up a breakfast roll from the vendor on the corner and carried on walking. Another thought popped into her head. She'd check out the Albanian online news pages – they would have reported a serious road accident and named the locality if not the victims.

The red-brick building with its arched entrance came into view. Roza waited for a gap in the traffic so she could cross the road. A girl of about her age wearing faded floral leggings and a baggy t-shirt was coming her way, struggling with bulging carrier bags. If she wasn't careful, she'd . . .

'Hey!' Roza bent down to rub her leg. The girl had nearly knocked her off her feet.

One of the bags split and carrots and potatoes spilled out, rolling towards the gutter.

The girl dropped to her knees with a groan, wheezing and mumbling swear words Roza had heard her brother use. She was Albanian.

'Oh no! Please help me,' she carried on, speaking English with a heavy accent. 'My mother will kill me if I don't go back with everything on her list.'

Roza squatted down. Thin scars twisted from the girl's forehead to the corner of her mouth.

In a heartbeat, the girl was back on her feet and leaning out over the kerb. Before Roza had a chance to register what was happening, a dark car with wheels the size of a tractor and blacked-out windows squealed to a stop and strong arms bundled her into the back.

Chapter Thirty-One

THE VEHICLE SWUNG INTO the torrent of traffic.

Slewed across the back seat, Roza tugged frantically at the door handle. With her other hand she thumped the window, screaming for help.

'Shut up.' Next to her, the man in khaki shorts who'd pushed her in, manhandled her into a sitting position. 'And don't even think about trying to get out.' He was long and bony with red hair that stood up like iron filings and there was a sing-song lilt to his voice.

The girl who had tricked her was settled in the passenger seat in front, wheezing as though she'd run a race. She jerked her head round to look at Roza.

'Good work, Snakeface.' The guard plastered a strip of coarse material across Roza's mouth. A hood followed, thick and tight. Everything was black; the voices muffled.

The car picked up speed and careered around one corner after another. It was like the chase to the bus station all over again. Roza was thrown against the seat. The next moment, they were stationary. At traffic lights? Surely people in other cars would be able to see her.

No, they wouldn't! Not with those blacked-out windows.

Roza's throat tightened. Even with the hood on there was no escaping the stench of sweat and cigarette smoke. It made her want to retch. She swallowed back the bile. She had been set up by that girl and, wherever they were taking her, there wasn't a thing she could do about it. She needed to stay calm.

Ten or fifteen minutes of driving in a straight line, then the driver swung hard to the left. The way the car was bouncing up and down it must be a track rutted with potholes. There was no traffic noise here, only the drone of a low plane passing overhead. Roza thrashed about, groping for something to hold on to. The bacon roll she'd had for breakfast felt like it was sloshing around in the tea she'd drunk. Suddenly, with a dip that sent her slamming against the window, the car crunched to a halt.

The Sing-Song guard hauled her out by her coat sleeve. Gravel crunched beneath her feet as he shoved her forward.

Bleeping noises followed, the whoosh of a door opening – they were inside an echoey space that reminded Roza of arriving at Ridley Road for the first time.

Without warning he whipped off her hood and gag.

She blinked, adjusting her eyes. There was a staircase to the left, a wide landing above. Where was he taking her?

'Start climbing!'

Roza hesitated. The other girl was already on her way up.

'Now!'

At the top, he tore off Roza's backpack. Her phone hit the floor with a thud. 'What's this then?' The guard picked it up and turned it over.

'Hey! That's mine,' Roza cried out.

'Pretty! Do nicely for my kid this will. Keeps on at me for one of these she does.'

A man with skinny legs and dressed in a neon orange tracksuit bounded up the stairs. Around his neck, a gold chain spelled out his name – *Vinny*.

'What use will she have for that Rusty? Livin' on some Welsh mountain with a load of sheep.'

The Welshman was rifling through Roza's bag now. Chuckling to himself as he held up the knickers and t-shirts she'd stuffed in at the last moment. 'Knew you'd be staying a while then.'

A drawer rolled open. She swung round in time to see her backpack being swallowed up into a filing cabinet.

'Where you been anyway, Vin, you lazy arse? You should have been here half hour ago. Get them into the holding room.'

'Been a hold up moving the other cargo on,' Vinny muttered. 'OK you two.'

He caught the top of the other girl's arm and hustled them both into a room on the far side of the stairs. The floor was bare and there was no light to see by, only thin strips of brightness around the blind

Roza shuffled up against the far wall and hugged her arms around her. There was no heat either but at least they hadn't taken her coat.

The other girl sank to the floor in the opposite corner, her head buried between her knees. She reminded Roza of a smaller version of Stefanie, with her deep fringe and raven-black hair. She started humming, a tuneless noise bracketed by laboured in-breaths.

Roza lifted her voice and spoke in Albanian. 'Where are we? Do you know?'

No reply.

'At least tell me what we are doing here? What will they do to us?'

Was she in a trance?

'You tricked me today! Are you working for them? Tell me! What is this place?'

When the girl didn't reply, Roza jammed her fingers into her ears.

Who were these men with their rough voices, locking her up? What were they going to do with her? Tears rose like water coming to the boil. It wasn't fair. They'd taken everything – her hard-earned money, her phone, even her backpack. She'd never find Michael Monette now. As for getting back to Albania . . .

A wave of exhaustion fell on her like a fog. She pulled a scrappy tissue from her pocket and wiped her nose. Ylli's blanket scrap was there too. She closed her eyes, fingering its soft edges, willing herself to stay calm.

When she awoke, the room was properly dark. It was colder too, and she was desperate to pee.

As she stood up and rubbed her arms, a tube light on the ceiling flickered. The Sing-Song guard was standing in the doorway. He pointed across the landing. 'Don't take all day about it.'

The other girl was staring dully into the distance when Roza came out. It was the first chance Roza had had to look at her properly. Suddenly it came to her. She was the older girl on the plane with Dori all those months back. Only then she'd had a fuller face and her long braids would have hidden any scars.

'OK Rust, I'll take it from here.' Vinny was back. 'Her Majesty wants to see this one in her office first.' He cocked his head towards Roza.

Ordering them back into the same room, he emptied the contents of a plastic carrier bag on to the floor. A few sandwiches curling at the edges, a bottle of water, some loose biscuits. As soon as he'd gone, the girl pounced on the food. She clawed at it like an animal, cramming it into her mouth as if she hadn't been fed for days. Perhaps she hadn't. Roza knelt down and scooped up the scraps.

'There are no regular mealtimes.' Biscuit crumbs sprayed from the girl's mouth. Her voice was stronger than Roza expected. 'You take what you can. Other girls arrive later.'

Others? 'How many?'

'There are never enough blankets, that's all I know.'

'Where are they now?' Roza asked, not sure she wanted to hear the answer.

'Bars, parlours. Some begging.'

'What kind of work at the bars?'

The girl threw her a dead-eyed look.

Roza gulped. *Sex workers? Would she be forced to do that too?*

The girl lifted a hank of hair and jabbed at her scars.

'Not likely to put *me* on display, are they? You?' She waggled her hand. 'Perhaps?'

Chapter Thirty-Two

LATER THAT NIGHT, ROZA crouched behind the door as the other girls filed in. Most of them were dressed in skimpy tops which revealed far more than just their arms and shoulders. And skirts that barely covered their backsides.

There was a scrap for the last few blankets. Nobody seemed to notice Roza, the new girl, except one. Fourteen at the most, and with one of her front teeth missing, the girl snatched the cover Roza had bagged and took it to the other corner of the room.

Roza smothered a moan. She wasn't going to claim it back, get into a big fight and draw attention to herself. She huddled further into her coat. It would have to do.

'Move up, move up, it is full house tonight.'

A female guard stood at the door – hard-faced, toned biceps – punching the stragglers in the back with her truncheon. She reminded Roza of the female commando doll in Stefanie's Barbie collection.

There were over twenty of them packed into a room meant for two people at the most. The room stank – of sweat and unwashed clothes . . . and something else she couldn't bear to think about. Jozif's words played over and over in her head like a stuck record. *It will be far worse if Adelina gets rid of you.*

The other Albanian girl had taken a blanket and tucked herself into the far corner. She'd been seized by a fit of coughing earlier. Now she started with the humming noise again.

A gravelly voice called out, 'Shut up, Snakeface. Unless you want a kicking, like last time.'

Roza stiffened. Thank goodness, the girl had taken the hint.

When she woke a few hours later there was a line of artificial light filtering through the door. She clambered to her feet, picked her way over the legs of a couple of girls and squeezed through the gap. There was nobody around. It sounded as if everyone was downstairs.

She tiptoed to the window and lifted the edge of the blind. It was a clear night with a full moon. Street lights glowed in the distance and there was a faint hum of traffic. This must be the front of the house with the track below winding down to the road they had turned off. It was a long way to run without being spotted, even if you could make it outside in the first place.

A light sputtered to the left and went out. Seconds later it lit up again, staying on this time and illuminating the front of a house close by. Two stick-like figures – lanky young boys, she thought – were led through the front door and bundled into the mouth of a waiting van. She followed the rear lights as it bumped along to the end of the track.

'No peeping, girlie.'

Roza jumped.

It was Vinny. Seizing her arm, he forced it up behind her back. It was all she could do not to cry out.

'Got it?' He dangled the burning end of a cigarette no more than a centimetre from her face.

***

Daylight arrived. The female guard jabbed first Roza and then the humming girl with her truncheon and told them to use the bathroom. After they'd done so, she led them down the corridor.

'That's Tamara,' the girl whispered in Albanian. 'She is taking us to The Hole, I know it.' She pushed her elbows into her ribs as though she wanted to disappear inside herself.

They trailed the guard to a door on the same floor. After a single knock, Tamara pushed Roza inside.

At first glance, the room looked empty apart from a desk in the far corner stacked high with brown folders. There was a filing cabinet next to it. A mug and a packet of biscuits sat on a small tray on top.

Then Roza heard the rustle of papers and looked again. She blinked in disbelief. It was Dori, her diminutive figure just visible behind the desk, turning the pages of one of the files. Peering over her half-moon glasses, she steepled her fingers under the loose folds of her chin.

'Dear me,' she said, pursing her lips. 'I didn't think we'd be seeing one another again quite so soon.'

She was wearing another matching two-piece, in lilac this time. And the bracelet, of course. She got to her feet and slipped her arms into the padded jacket hanging on the back of her seat.

She looked Roza up and down. 'Your cousin didn't do a very good job of keeping you locked up, did she? Let's see if we can do any better.' Dori turned. Tamara was holding the door open. 'You will be working for me now. And just so we are clear about consequences . . .'

As Roza followed Dori towards the stairs, she heard humming. She paused outside the door next to the holding room. It had been open when they arrived yesterday – a store cupboard, less than a metre deep.

Tamara's truncheon pressed against her spine. 'Get moving!'
So that was what the girl meant by *The Hole*.

At the front door, Dori slipped her feet into outdoor shoes. She led Roza past a pile of builders' rubble to the back of the house where Rusty was wielding a shovel.

'Show her what happens to troublemakers, Rusty,' she said in an even voice. 'The ones who have tried to escape.'

He led the way between tall spiky grass and brambles. A path opened up, revealing two sets of footprints. Roza stumbled after him, missing her footing more than once. She glanced over her shoulder to see how far they had come. Behind her Dori waved a walking stick. 'Keep going.'

Finally, they stopped. With a mean smile, Rusty curled his index finger and summoned her forward. A thorny weed pricked her finger. Blood oozed out and she sucked it away. When she lifted her head, she thought her heart would stop. Less than a metre in front of her the ground was covered by a raised rectangle of earth. Apart from the weeds and the lack of a cross, it was no different from the grave the family had stood around when Sindi died.

Dori had caught up with them. She nodded at Rusty and he stepped to one side, pulling roughly at clumps of grass to reveal another two raised patches. Roza's legs shook. She sank to her knees. People were buried here? Girls, like her?

The guard sliced the earth with his spade and started digging. Her heart began pounding and wouldn't stop. They were going to kill her, maybe even bury her alive.

Dori folded her hands in front of her. 'It's always a matter of regret when we have to move people on. We don't do it out of choice. Best you know that at the outset. Try to escape and . . .'

Rusty stopped digging. She had been warned.

Chapter Thirty-Three

THEY WENT BACK INSIDE. The humming girl was sitting cross-legged by the front door.

Roza had no words. And if the other girl had any, she wouldn't make herself heard through that whistly breathing. It reminded her of Lorik. Did this girl have asthma too?

A dark saloon pulled up, music pounding from inside. Vinny slid out and made them get in. Where were they going now? Roza's heart was thumping but she squared her shoulders. She had to stay strong, show no fear, put those graves out of her mind. It wouldn't happen to her; she would make sure of that.

There were no hoods or masks this time. The car made its way the short disrtance to the building she'd seen lit up last night. From the outside it looked identical to the holding house – tall and flat-fronted and plastered with white pebble-dash. Blinds hung at every window. Even the security pads were in the exact same position – on the right of wooden front doors.

Vinny hustled them out of the car and across a carpet of chippings. 'Come on then, girlies. Let's get you to work.'

She'd hoped to catch a look at the numbers he keyed in but he made them turn away. *Could he read Roza's mind?*

Inside Roza slapped a hand over her nose at the sweet, sickly smell.

As they climbed the stairs, the other girl started to wheeze more loudly.

'Dori can't stand her,' Vinny said cheerfully. 'Didn't reckon on her being such a weakling.'

'She needs to see a doctor,' said Roza.

'Yeah, and my name's Santa Claus.'

He pulled out a bunch of keys and unlocked the first door on the left.

Row upon row of green plants lined rough wooden tables in a room that ran from the front to the back of the house. The heat was suffocating. Roza fanned her face.

'Welcome to The Farm, girlies. Just growing a few medicinal herbs.' Vinny grinned, showing a mouthful of yellowing teeth, and waggled two garden-sized watering cans in their faces. He rubbed the leaves gently between his fingers. 'These little lovelies need watering every day. That'll fill your morning. There'll be *big* trouble if you let the plants dry out. Or give them too much water. Mug's the expert, he'll come to check regular like. He'll expect everything to be *hunky dory*.' He jabbed Roza in the ribs. 'Dori! Get it? And the lights . . . mustn't forget those.'

Roza blinked at the saucer-shaped lamps hanging from the ceiling. So that was where the heat was coming from.

Vinny stooped to lift a handful of cables. 'Careful o' these. You trip and make the lights go out . . .' He shook his head in a worried kind of way. 'And the floors'll need sweeping. Under the tables too.'

On and on he droned until a noise blasted from his phone and he hurried out.

Roza followed him across the landing to the room at the front. He'd shut the door. Did she dare go in after him? The air felt thick. She wanted to fling open a window but they were all locked.

She gave the door a tap and opened it bit by bit. Vinny was lowering himself into a blue reclining seat, the only piece of furniture in the room. Sweet wrappings, an ashtray overflowing with cigarette stubs and a pile of magazines sat in an untidy pile underneath. He glanced up from his phone.

'It's far too hot to sleep in the farm, and the bright lights . . .'

'Who said anything about sleeping here? Do the job proper and you'll be taken back to the holding house. Taxi service every night.'

'What about food? We haven't eaten . . .'

'You're a cocky one, ain't you.' He looked her up and down. 'You earn your grub here, girlie. We'll see if you and Snakface do enough to deserve any.'

Roza went to use the toilet. There was a bath in there too but it was filled with bags of compost.

When she came out, Vinny was snoring. This was her chance to look around, see what opportunties there were to escape.

She tried the door next to the bathroom. It was unlocked, but difficult to open because of the boxes of light bulbs, plastic pots, cables and other equipment packed behind it.

There was one other door on the first floor. Narrow, with a keypad on the right, it matched the cupboard the girl had been locked up in at the holding house.

Roza tiptoed downstairs. Most of the ground floor was one huge open space with no furniture. Roza peered through the blinds at the back. Builders' tools and other discarded equipment littered the rough ground outside. Broken bricks, and even a cement mixer with weeds growing out of it. As far as she could see, apart from a short line of trees on the left edge the land was no different from the back of the holding house – covered with tall grass and wild plants.

She heard footsteps above her, smelled fresh cigarette smoke. Vinny was on his way downstairs. The only place to hide was the kitchen.

Roza held her breath as he moved across the hall. The door slammed and an engine started outside. She opened cupboards and then the fridge. Hopefully Vinny had gone to get them something to eat. There was nothing here apart from a few cans of lager and half a packet of stale biscuits.

She opened a door at the other end and stepped into what looked like an empty garage. It jutted out from the rest of the house. It was cold and damp like her cell in Ridley Road but it was a relief from the heat. She tried the big retractable door on the off chance it would budge. But no, of course it didn't.

Trudging back upstairs she dropped into Vinny's chair. Rain had swept in overnight and dark clouds hung heavy, blocking the long view. One of the magazines slid out. There were pictures of naked girls on the front cover. *Ugh!* She stuffed it back. They were the last thing she needed to see.

She groaned and cradled her head between her hands. She wouldn't *be* here if she hadn't been so stubborn. Turning down offers of help. Not just from Jason. Mr Joe had reached out to her. Wendy too.

Stop it! This was no time to wallow in self-pity. Vinny could be back any minute.

Back in the farm, Roza went to the sink and filled the empty can.

The other girl was sitting on the floor again. 'Finished the grand tour?'

'You've been here before?'

'Oh yes.' The girl spread her arms. 'They used to keep us here before we went begging.'

Did she know about the graves?

'Tell me your name. Mine is Roza.'

'I am Hanna. You were on the flight from Tirana.'

Roza nodded. 'Let's divide the the plants, then we'll each have a section to look after,' she said briskly. 'Less chance we'll miss any that way.' She drew an imaginary line across the centre of the tables. 'I'll cover the ones closer to the door.'

When Hanna didn't respond, Roza said, 'Look, I don't like it any more than you do but if we slip up they will only make life harder for us. Playing by their rules will be best. To start with anyway. Buy us some time to work on a plan.'

Hanna got up and trudged to the sink, rolling her eyes.

She was so thin and flimsy. Like tissue paper. No point in expecting any help from her.

'There were young boys here before us. I saw them in the night.' Roza tipped up the can to check the pouring rose was positioned properly. She told Hanna how she nearly paid the price for her night wanderings with a cigarette burn.

'Why would you do that?'

'I intend to do everything I can to get away,' Roza said with as much bravado as she could manage. 'I just need to work out a plan.'

'So you keep saying. Wait till you have been here long as me. See how you feel then about putting up a fight.'

'How long *have* you been here?'

Hanna lifted her shoulders. 'Five, six months? I don't know. There's no way to measure the time.' She put her can down. 'They made me do it, you know. Trick you yesterday. I heard them say you escaped from a house in Oxford.'

'I don't suppose you had any choice.'

The front door bleeped. Vinny's light footsteps sounded on the stairs. He grinned at them from the doorway. 'That's the ticket! Good girlies, doing what they're told.'

He sidled up to Hanna. Her can was almost full and she was struggling to hold it straight so that the water poured in a steady stream. Roza glanced across from her own section. One trough of plants was already sitting in a pool.

Hanna jumped as Vinny wrenched the can from her. Water splashed over her feet as he pushed her roughly against the wall. Struggling to stay upright she tripped over a length of cable, pulling the plug out of its socket. The light went out.

'Oi, you weren't payin' attention to what I said, were you?' He kicked the cable under the table and forced the plug back in.

Hanna was on the floor. There was a cut on her forehead and her breath was coming in sharp gasps. Vinny grabbed the front of her t-shirt and hauled her to her feet.

'Don't hurt her,' Roza shouted. 'You can see . . .'

'She's not well.' Vinny feigned a girl's voice. 'Yeah, you said.' His eyes narrowed to slits. 'And don't we all know it. Useless piece of trash. Don't know why Dori don't finish her off like the others.'

Show her what we do with troublemakers. Roza tightened her arms around her waist to stop them trembling.

Vinny planted himself in front of her, pressing his hands down hard on her shoulders.

'*You* remember everything I said, don't you? Make sure she does too. I'll be holding you responsible.' His face relaxed. He was grinning as he pointed to the carrier bag by the door. 'Grub for later, girlies. Don't eat it all at once.'

Chapter Thirty-Four

BY THE END OF the first week Roza was used to ticking off her jobs for the day. Water the plants, check the lamps, keep the cables tidy, sweep the floor. Only now she had another one to add to the list. Check Hanna's work.

Today had gone without a hitch. They'd finished the plants, the floor was clean and no bulbs had blown. Stepping gingerly over the cables, Roza joined Hanna on the floor.

'Let's finish this before they come to collect us. Who knows when that will be?' She tipped out the thin pasty Vinny had left them and tore it in half.

Now she knew Roza wasn't going to fight her for the food, Hanna chewed at a slower pace. 'Thank you for your kindness the other day. It is unknown here.'

'You don't need to keep thanking me.' Roza nibbled at the cold pastry. There was hardly any meat. 'Is your head OK now?'

Hanna touched her forehead. 'One more lump to add to the others,' she said with a weak smile.

Roza couldn't be lighthearted about it. Either Hanna had missed Vinny's comment about Dori finishing her off or she didn't want to hear, but it had been ringing in Roza's ears ever since.

'Does Vinny often behave like that?' she said.

Hanna shrugged. 'Sometimes he's OK. Rusty's always a thug.' She shivered as though some memory had returned to haunt her. 'Whenever we were on the streets begging, he used to make us kneel, you know like you make a dog sit up and beg. The ground cut hard into our knees. He'd make us stay for hours. It was the worst time.' She licked a finger and dabbed at the remaining flakes of pastry. 'What about you? How did they treat you in Oxford?'

Roza kept it short – the story of her time with the Brakas; the abuse she had suffered. Hanna didn't ask how or why she had been trafficked and Roza had no intention of telling her – admitting her father had sold her, saying the words out loud.

'It wasn't all bad though. What's it been like here for you?'

To Roza's relief the conversation turned back to Hanna.

'Dori made me snitch on the other girls when I was first brought here. She called me her *bottom bitch*. It's why they hate me so much. Now she has me locked up in The Hole whenever she feels like it. Just to remind me who is boss.'

Roza shuddered. Once in the dirty cupboard at the Brakas had been bad enough. 'And the humming?'

'Happy songs from my childhood. It calms me. My asthma gets worse if I freak out.

'Where are you from?' Roza asked.

'A little village just outside Tirana. I was in the school choir. You like singing?'

'Not really.' Roza allowed herself a small smile. 'My friend Stefanie got us into trouble making up rude words to the songs, and the music teacher threw us out.'

Hanna shifted closer to the lamp and curled up underneath. 'What did you mean when you said *it wasn't all bad* in Oxford?'

Roza told her about working in *Rainbow*, Wendy's kindness and how well she had eaten there. It was a relief to talk about something nice for a moment. One story led to another and, without meaning to, she found herself talking about Jason.

'He was your boyfriend?'

Roza's cheeks flamed. Their day out in London had certainly felt like a date. 'I suppose so, but not for long. Just before I managed to escape from Oxford, I badly needed his help. I sent him a text. He didn't reply.' She huffed. 'Do you know the English expression? *Stand on your own two feet.* That way no one can let you down.'

Hanna sat up. 'Perhaps he didn't get the message?'

'Of course he did. He just didn't like it that I . . .' Roza waved her hand dismissively. 'Oh, it doesn't matter. It's all in the past now.'

Hanna pulled her hair back and leaned forward to mop up the crumbs left from the pasty.

'Those scars,' Roza ventured. She paused. *Was it OK to ask?* 'Did Dori . . . ?'

The girl coughed out a hard laugh. 'No. This was a road accident when I was eleven. My uncle was drunk.'

Her eyes glazed over.

'Hanna?'

There was a long pause before she shook herself. 'Sorry. I have holes in my memory.'

'You were telling me about Dori,' Roza said slowly.

'She sent a woman to our village who pretended to be an aid worker. She said she was married to a plastic surgeon and he would fix my face. My mother knew I would never find a husband so she gave this woman all her savings and sent me away with her.' Hanna's face crumpled. 'The woman told Mami she would bring me home *a different girl.*'

Roza's heart was thumping. *A village outside Tirana.* 'What was she like, this woman?'

'Smart clothes, nice car. Older than Mami. I never thought she looked like an aid worker. She had a funny way of talking, the way she said her 'r's.'

Aunty Sade.

Roza seized Hanna's hand. 'You *will* go home. We will escape from here – from Dori – both of us.'

Hanna pulled away. Colour flared in her cheeks. 'Don't say that when it's not true. You're crazy to think we will ever get away from that woman!'

A few days later, Roza found a penknife wedged between two of the plant pots. She tucked it inside her jeans pocket. It would do to score notches along the edge of one of the tables to keep track of the days and weeks.

Hanna told her she was wasting her time but all Roza knew was the moment she stopped hoping, stopped believing there was a way out of this place, she would lose the will to live.

She decided to set herself memory challenges. Repeating her times tables, remembering dates from the Albanian wars and the Enver Hoxhe era. Anything to keep her brain active. She even attempted to recite passages of poetry she once knew by heart.

Not that she got very far with that. She could still picture the verses on the pages of the anthology Babi had bought her last Christmas. But the hunger made it hard to concentrate.

And she was anxious about her family. She went to sleep with them. She woke up with them. Before, there had been no doubt in Roza's mind that Adelina was lying – that the people she cared about most in the world were still alive and that one day they would all be reunited.

But now their faces were out of focus, like photos fading with the passage of time. Maybe Adelina had told the truth and they were dead after all.

Chapter Thirty-Five

ON DAY TWENTY VINNY produced a tape measure. He lined it up against plants from each section and, muttering to himself, wrote down the results. Hanna stood by the door, chewing her nails and humming tunelessly under her breath.

He closed his little notebook. 'Nice work, girlies,' Vinny said. 'Make sure you keep it up.'

Roza let out a silent breath. Checking Hanna's work was paying off.

He left for the next room. A minute later, they could hear his phone trilling, as it did at the same time every morning.

'He must be playing games,' Roza whispered. 'Or gambling.'

'He gives me the creeps,' Hanna said later, when he had gone for the day. 'You never know what mood he will be in. Not that he is the worst of them. When we got off the plane . . .'

Roza put her can down and listened as Hanna recounted her arrival in the UK.

From Heathrow, Hanna had been driven to a restaurant in Reading and told she would be working for Dori's brother.

'A few weeks later, when there was no one around, I ran out and flagged down a car. A woman drove me to a police station.

They put me in a hostel and I was due to move to Bristol, but Dori's man, Toska, found out where I was staying. He beat me badly and brought me here.' She picked in an absent-minded way at a hole in her jumper. 'Dori had me cleaning her office for a while until she said I was not good enough to do even that. If I had not suffered that accident, would I even be here now?'

Hanna had said the same thing, just yesterday. Roza looked away. She wasn't going to upset her by telling her how much she repeated herself.

'I think Dori wants to be rid of me. I'm no use to her and she worries what I remember.'

Roza sat forward. 'What do you mean?'

Hanna tapped the side of her head and gave a grim laugh. 'Names, places – details the police would be interested in.'

'Dori's the head honcho then?'

'Oh yes. She has people all over the place. That woman who recruited me, she is only one. Romania, Bulgaria, Poland . . .'

Aunty Sade works for Dori. Roza had assumed it was the other way around.

But she didn't want to talk about Aunty. 'The floor is a mess,' she said quickly. 'Have you swept under that table behind you? There's a pile of dead leaves.'

Hanna sighed and got to her feet. Roza tidied one of the tables and moved some of the straggly-looking plants from Hanna's section to the back. Vinny was less likely to see them there.

'Hey, look.' A small round bottle covered with dried leaves and dust balls sat in the palm of her hand.

'Nail polish.' Roza lifted it to the light. The bottle was almost full. Of course. Girls had been held in this room before.

'My sister and I used to paint each other's nails,' Hanna said wistfully. 'She worked at the local store. They gave her discount so she bought many colours!' They traded smiles and Hanna raised her eyebrows. 'It might be fun.'

'Will you do mine later then?' said Roza.

Hanna was waiting for her in the kitchen. 'Welcome to Hanna's Nail Bar,' she said, putting on a French accent. 'Would Mademoiselle care to be seated?'

She'd found two candle stubs in a drawer and lit them with the matches Vinny kept for his cigarettes. There was no bulb in the ceiling and the candles gave off an eerie glow.

Roza giggled and slid on to one of the chairs. It was such a weird thing to be doing here. She held out a hand, her fingers splayed.

Perching on the edge of the table, Hanna leaned forward and applied the scarlet liquid down each nail with sweeping strokes.

Roza watched in awe. 'I always make such a mess of mine.'

Hanna's face was screwed up in concentration.

'After we get away from here you should open your own nail bar,' Roza said. She lifted her eyes waiting for a reaction.

Hanna didn't reply. She tipped her head. 'Look, I've missed a bit there. The light is terrible.' She dipped the brush into the bottle again and held it up.

A drop landed on the table. It could have been blood.

Roza pulled her hand back and blew hard on her nails. 'Thanks, that'll do. They're fab.'

They were halfway up the stairs when they heard Vinny stumble in through the front door. He was talking to himself, getting his words mixed up.

Hanna skittered to the top and and slipped the bottle into her pocket.

Roza glanced over her shoulder. 'He sounds a bit worse for wear to me.'

Vinny lurched towards them, a sour smell of beer on his breath. He dropped a carrier bag on to the floor. There was a half-eaten packet of egg sandwiches inside.

'Come and keep your Uncle Vin company, girlies,' he said. 'We'll have a carpet supper together.'

He settled himself into his usual chair and thrust his phone at Hanna. 'Sit down, sit down! See if you can bring your Uncle Vin a bit of luck tonight.'

He told her to click on one of the two figure numbers in gold on the screen. Hanna gave the key a tentative tap.

An idea was taking shape in Roza's head. When Hanna's eyes flicked nervously at her, Roza nodded at her to keep going.

Vinny swung his can up to his lips, splashing beer over his tracksuit bottoms.

With any luck alcohol would make him sleepy, like it did with Babi. They'd have the chance to snatch his phone and dial 999. And the police would race over here, blue lights flashing . . .

As long as the phone signal gave their location away. Roza wasn't so sure about that bit.

'Your go.' Hanna passed the phone over like it was a piece of dynamite.

Roza pressed a few random numbers. The phone trilled and gold pound signs lit up the screen.

'Yes!' Vinny grabbed it back from her and beamed. 'Twenty-five quid! My lucky stars, that's what you two are!'

The empty beer can rolled off his lap and on to the floor.

'Do you want another?' Roza signalled to Hanna to fetch it from the fridge.

Vinny's head lolled forward, then jerked up again. 'C'mon, c'mon, there's more to win,' he said, his voice drowsy.

His head tipped back and didn't come up again. He began to snore.

Roza clasped her hands against her chest and counted slowly to five. His legs were sprawled out like a pair of open scissors, his mobile resting on his crotch. She shifted her body weight forward. *No sudden movements.* One twitch of his leg and the phone would slide on to the floor. The noise would be certain to wake him.

Hanna reappeared in the doorway. Roza put a finger to her lips. She edged her hand closer to the phone.

Neither of them heard the car outside until its headlights were sliding across the ceiling. A horn blasted twice.

Roza leapt to her feet.

Vinny wiped a thread of drool from his chin and jerked upright.

Roza hadn't reached the door before his hand was on her shoulder. His fingers dug into her flesh. She choked back a yelp.

'Don't think I don't know your little game, girlie. Just you remember, Uncle Vin's got his eye on you.'

Chapter Thirty-Six

SHE HAD A DREAM that night where she and Hanna did manage to snatch the phone. Only it wasn't the police who answered when she rang – it was Babi. Going to live with Adelina had been a terrible mistake, he told her. He'd come and find her; do whatever it took. So Roza waited and waited outside the cannabis house but when a taxi pulled up it was Tamara who stepped out, laughing and wagging her truncheon like a hideous witch in a fairytale. Roza woke screaming and was told to shut up.

In the morning a new guard with big teeth was outside in the car, chuntering into his phone.

Roza and Hanna got in.

'Where d'you think Vinny is?' asked Roza.

'Probably on the streets with the girls. Dori moves people around all the time.'

'I haven't seen the guard with the big belly either. Not since I was in Oxford.'

'Toska, you mean.' Hanna gave a thin smile. 'Dori probably sacked him for letting you get away. Nobody gets a second chance here.'

The car stopped. The Weasel opened the car door and jostled them through a blast of cold air towards the cannabis house. 'Stand there. And look away.'

He cupped the scrap of paper in his palm, frowning at the figures. When he got it wrong twice, he swore loudly.

He was trying all the pockets of his biker jacket now – and with his back to them. Could they make a run for it? Flag down a car on the main road? But Hanna would never make it. She'd done nothing this morning and already she was short of breath.

The second scrap of paper floated to the ground and landed on Roza's trainer. *3110.* The Weasel snatched it up. 'Don't think of doing anything clever,' he stuttered, putting on a rough voice. 'There'll be a . . . guard outside all day.'

There wouldn't, of course. In six weeks, Roza had never seen one there.

She clutched Hanna's arm as soon as they were on their own. 'We can get out, run away. Not from the front, it's far too open and they probably have CCTV. But at the back there are places to hide – trees, bushes, long grass . . .'

'What? You are crazy,' Hanna replied. She turned to pick up her can. 'They will catch us and beat us. Or worse.'

'Then we won't let them catch us.' Roza grabbed Hanna by the shoulders. 'There's plenty of cover at the back and you know I'll help you. We can't be too far from shops and houses. Look!' She pointed to a tall apartment block in the distance. 'I'm not leaving you here, Hanna. This is too good a chance to pass up.'

'I would slow you up. You go, if you must.' Hanna spun the tap and pushed her can underneath.

Roza fetched her coat. Maybe it was for the best. On her own she would be able to move at speed. Once safe, she could raise the alarm for everybody else.

She didn't trust the police. Involving them meant she'd be caught up in the legal system she'd so far avoided. But she had no choice. Like Jason said, it wasn't just about her any more.

Jason. Roza said his name out loud. After four weeks, he must know she wasn't coming back. She blinked back tears and fastened the toggles on her coat. There was no time to think about him now.

'Paç fat,' Hanna hissed from the top of the stairs. *Good luck.*

Roza keyed in the numbers and felt the lock give way. Slowly she opened the door and looked across to the holding house. There was no one there.

She stepped outside. She was really going to do this.

She trod carefully through the bushes and brambles. But the thorny branches were thick and vicious and kept catching on her coat. Underfoot the ground, which was uneven to start with, became rougher and she had to negotiate pieces of broken brick and stones.

A voice echoed, a door slammed and a car roared into action. Roza clapped a hand over her heart, but the noise faded quickly. *Calm down.* Even supposing anyone was looking, she couldn't be seen from the house. She glanced back. She must be a good thirty metres away from the cannabis house now.

She continued along the flattened trail. In some places it was wide enough for two to walk side by side.

Then, without warning, the ground dropped, jarring her neck. Cold liquid pooled inside her shoes. *Stupid mistake!* She had to get back on to the path.

The slope was steep but not hard to find. She kept going as it widened then came to an abrupt end. In a deep patch of dried mud there were clear footprints. Two sets.

Her heart gave an uncomfortable thump as she ploughed on. *Not here too?* She forced herself onwards. Sure enough, there was a curved bank of earth. It was another grave. Only this time the soil was fresher and free from weeds.

Roza couldn't get away fast enough. A swift recce of the ground ahead decided it. *Go left.* The ground appeared flatter there. She'd go through the long grass easily enough.

Minutes later, it was obvious she'd made the wrong choice. Her shoes slid sideways in the mud as she fought to get a grip. When she threw her arms out in an attempt to stay upright, her foot twisted over. She yelled out in pain. Attempting to pull it free was fruitless. The boggy ground was sucking her down with the power of a Hoover nozzle. Panic rose in her chest. She fell forwards. Liquid mud seeped through her fingers and when she pushed her hands into the ground to raise herself on to her knees, they sank out of sight.

Minutes passed. If she moved, she was sure to sink deeper into the mire. Roza's arms ached and her breath was growing ragged.

Stay calm. And think!

There was a scattering of low-growing woody plants around her. One no more than a metre away. She strained her right arm forward. Once. Twice. On the third attempt she felt her foot shift. Enough to stretch a few more centimetres and wrap her fingers around the knobbly stem of the plant. Now for her left arm. She would need both of them to heave herself out. Roza lunged foward and, pulling with all her might, felt the suck of the mud release her foot.

The drag back to the higher ground was child's play by comparison. Now all she had to do was make a path through the long grass and keep the swampy area to the right at a distance. She sat down to rest for a few minutes and wiped the mud away from her mouth. Her clothes were caked in the stuff, her fingernails torn and filthy. The only other time she could remember being caught in mud like this was at the village swamp. She and Lorik playing, the summer before she moved into third grade.

A sudden leap of understanding hit her like a punch to the stomach. It wasn't long grass she was staring at. It was marsh reeds. They had been there all the time and she hadn't recognised them.

Never play at the swamp. Even now she could hear the terror in Babi's voice when he found the two of them, the grip of his fingers as he dragged them home, telling them about the little boy who had drowned in the marshes a couple of years before.

Roza peeled away the memory. She couldn't stop shivering. The air temperature had plummeted and it was only a matter of time before she was reported missing. What might they do to Hanna?

The only other option was making for the potholed track and flagging down a car on the main road. To do that, she'd not only have to retrace her steps but walk another hundred metres in full view of the holding house. Cautiously, Roza hoisted herself on to her feet. Pain speared through her ankle. She toppled against the sturdy plant she'd been clinging to and started to sob.

There was only one way to go. Back to the farm.

Roza limped in, teeth chattering, mud clinging to every part of her. Hanna helped Roza out of her clothes.

'We can soak these in the sink. Then hang them under the lamps to dry.' She had chosen the best moment to take charge.

The Weasel returned later with some food. Roza hid in the bathroom, cocooned in a dirty old towel. She heard Hanna making excuses for her. *Bellyache. Giving her the runs. Back and forth to the toilet all day.*

Roza held her breath. Vinny might have demanded proof but the Weasel couldn't get out fast enough.

'Aren't you going to eat something?' Hanna peered into the bag he had dropped by the door.

Roza shivered, tousling her hair under a lamp.

'At least you tried,' Hanna chirped. 'There's a bit of naan bread left over from someone's curry.' She broke it in two and offered one piece to Roza.

Roza's heart was going full pelt. 'I *tried*. Is that all you can say?'

The bread hung in Hanna's hand. 'Of course I *tried*,' said Roza, as though she was explaining something glaringly obvious to a small child. 'How else will we get out of this place if we don't? You want to, you know you do. Underneath all that fear.'

'I just want to stay alive,' Hanna said in a small voice. 'I tried to get away before, remember? It's too hard. I cannot do it again.'

'You call this being *alive*? They prey on our fear, Dori and the guards. And it's each girl for herself. Every night, fighting over the blankets, the food, a space on the floor. For an hour this morning I tasted freedom – the blue sky, fresh air in my lungs. And until it all went wrong it felt good. I was trying with all my might to do something that would make a difference for us.'

'Us?'

'Yes! And if you weren't so full of thinking about yourself, you might see it too. You have been through hard times. So have I. So have all the other girls. It's not a competition. Yes, I was going for the *both* of us. If I'd managed to get to safety, don't you think I'd have told the police that you and twenty-five others were here too?'

Roza clamped her hands under her armpits. Her throat was so thick she could hardly squeeze the words out.

'D'you know what? You are right. There is no escape out of this place. I give up. Dori can do what she likes with me.'

Chapter Thirty-Seven

Roza's ankle was swollen for a week. And painful for longer than that. Hanna tried to do all the watering for a few days but the job was too much for one person and they couldn't afford to neglect any plants. 'Thanks, but no thanks,' Roza said. She'd just have to carry on.

As she trudged back and forth to the taps, she felt herself sinking as surely as if she had stepped into those marsh reeds. Fifty days they'd been at the cannabis house – she'd counted the notches that morning. It must be the middle of November by now.

She caught sight of her reflection in the window. How scraggy she had become. Pale and thin and shapeless. Her jeans hung from her waist and her breasts had stopped growing, she was convinced of it. Tasting freedom, finding out whether her family were alive – it wasn't going to happen and she'd better face up to it.

All morning she dragged her feet. She snapped at Hanna when she found a whole tray of plants dry and shrivelled.

'These haven't been watered for days.' She held one up. 'If Vinny sees . . .'

Hanna took them from her without a word and hid them under the table at the back. She'd nurture them back to health, she promised.

That night, a story circulated in the holding house about two girls being beaten by clients at a local truck-stop. One of the girls who had witnessed the incident started to sob. Roza held her hand and tried to comfort her.

When they talked the next morning, Hanna was less concerned. 'Tamara moved them out. Not to upset the others. It happens sometimes.'

'They weren't taken to hospital?' Roza said.

'Are you serious?'

'What will happen to them? Will they come back?'

Hanna shrugged. 'Dori will probably move them on.'

'*Move them on.* You mean, make them disappear?'

'What are you saying?'

'Nothing.'

Roza left to go to the toilet. She locked the door and sat on the edge of the bath. She still couldn't bring herself to talk to Hanna about the graves.

'They move girls on sometimes,' Hanna said when Roza returned.

She'd been thinking about it.

'Like Marta. She was kind to me. But, like you, feisty – always answering back. One day, she just didn't return with the others.'

There was a whining noise outside. Roza went to the window. A car she didn't recognise – sleek and metallic – was parked up close to the building. To avoid being seen? The gravel crunched and a low rumble of voices followed.

'I can only see one of them – a man, I think. There's someone in the car too.' She turned to Hanna. 'Who do you think it is? They must see the alarm. And what's here to steal anyway?'

Hanna shuffled over to join her. She shrugged. 'Dori has been in business for years. She must have made enemies in that time.'

A thump on one of the full-length windows at the back made them both jump.

'But to come in daylight. Whoever it is must know the routine. That the other girls have been driven off to the parlours by now so none of the guards are on site. Wait here.'

Roza tiptoed downstairs. She crept to the back window and peered between two slats of the blind. She froze. Someone was there cupping their eyes to the other side of the glass. She couldn't make out a face. Had they seen hers?

The next morning, Rusty arrived early at the holding house.

'Get up!' He prodded Roza then Hanna with his foot. 'Mug's on his way. See how the plants are doing.'

The expert on cultivating cannabis. Roza cast an anxious eye around the farm as soon as Rusty let them in.

If Vinny was here now, he would have been fussing, pulling off dead leaves – and there were plenty on Hanna's side – making them wipe down the tables, getting them to crawl underneath to sweep up any bits of rubbish. He was supposed to come every day but they hadn't seen him for weeks. Rusty seemed unbothered.

Mug was a squat man with a square head and surprisingly clean hands and fingernails. He moved slowly between the tables, examining each pot with meticulous attention.

'Nice little earner this, Mug,' Rusty said in a conversational tone. 'Don't know why Dori didn't cotton on to it sooner.'

'Not if they all go the same way as this one.' Mug frowned and raised a particularly sad-looking looking pot from Hanna's side up to the light. 'You been watering at night? Encourages mould. Morning's the time. Gets the nutrients in.'

Roza's own section had suffered too, because of her ankle, but now she was looking closely, there were several more on Hanna's side well past reviving. The leaves looked diseased – dried up, curling in on themselves.

'This is no good.' The little man's eyes flashed at Hanna, and then at Roza. He lifted up another three pots in quick succession. 'It's all down to care*ful* watering and regular checking. This is care*less* work, that's what it is.' He tipped the contents on to the floor, one by one, crunching the plastic pots under his thick black boots. He eyeballed Rusty. 'You need to keep a closer eye on things, son. Dori won't be happy.'

Rusty raised his hands defensively. 'Talking to the wrong guy, Mug. Not my patch. Vinny's your man.'

'Where *is* Vinny?' Roza ventured when Mug had gone.

Rusty looked at her like she was dog dirt on the sole of his shoe. 'Lazy sod rang in sick again. Two days on the trot. Must've known Mug was coming today.' He spread his legs and folded his arms across his chest. 'Right! You heard what the man said. Get the place cleaned up. Your *boss* is gonna get both barrels from Dori when he's in next.'

As if something had jogged his memory, Rusty's hand went to his pocket.

He dangled Roza's phone in her face. 'Seeing my little girl tonight, I am. Birthday treat.' He clicked his tongue and ambled towards the stairs.

'You haven't left us anything to eat,' Roza called after him.

Rusty didn't break his stride. Wagging his finger above his head, he said, 'People have to earn their crust. No one ever teach you that?'

As soon as he was out of earshot Roza stared fiercely at Hanna. 'Great! Nothing to eat and all this mess to clear up.'

Hanna pinned her arms against her stomach and looked down at her trainers. 'It was only a few plants.'

'It was at least twenty and most of them were in your half! The earth was bone dry. How could you be so sloppy?' Roza barely recognised her own voice. 'Vinny will get into trouble and take it out on us. If we're going to find a way out of here, we need to keep him sweet, not irritate him. Can't you at least remember that?'

She stamped down the stairs. Away from the heat. Away from the dazzling lights. Away from Hanna.

Her fingers jabbed uselessly at the keypad on the front door but the numbers didn't work any more. Roza thumped it with her fist. The code must have changed.

She paced the ground floor trying to ignore the nagging ache in her stomach. At the back of a kitchen cupboard there was a half-eaten tin of boiled sweets, dusty and stuck together. They must have been there for months. Without thinking any more about it she stuffed the lot into her mouth. Sticky saliva ran down her chin. She didn't care. It was worth it for the sugar rush.

She pulled a seat out and sat down at the table. Guilt emptied over her like hot ashes. It was the second time in two weeks she'd taken her fury out on Hanna. She saw the way the girl struggled, staring at the plants sometimes as if she hadn't a clue what she was supposed to be doing. She couldn't help it – Roza knew that.

She rested her head on her hands. After a few minutes, she nodded off. When she came to her neck was stiff. But her anger had passed. As if the plug had been pulled on a sinkful of dirty water.

She stretched her arms. There was a hole coming in the sleeve of her sweatshirt. She tucked the running thread inside and breathed out a sigh. Whether she liked it or not, she and Hanna were stuck here together.

Upstairs she could hear a tap spurting. Floorboards squeaked. Footsteps padded back and forth. Roza glanced out of the window. A robin, his breast puffed up and scarlet, was pulling berries off a bush.

A rustling sound in the doorway made her look around. Hanna was there.

'I didn't know where you were.' The small voice again. She still looked unsure about meeting Roza's eye. '*When spiders' webs unite, they can tie up a lion*. Do you know that proverb?'

Roza got the gist. At least she thought she did. Something about working together to reach an impossible goal? She smiled to herself. It reminded her of Mrs Cicu. She was always going on about the importance of teamwork.

Hanna wrung her hands like a wet dishrag. 'Everything was bad enough and I've just made things worse, haven't I? You look like you're ready to give up.' She inhaled, a long slow breath that seemed to come up from the soles of her feet. 'Maybe we won't get out of here, but we can try, can't we? Together?'

Roza stood up, shifting from foot to foot. 'Yes. And I'm sorry too. What I said – I was out of order.' She lifted her eyes and met Hanna's. Nervously they smiled at one another.

'I'll paint *your* nails tonight if you like,' Roza said. 'I think there's just enough left in the bottle.'

The driver was very late picking them up that night. The other girls were already in the holding room by the time they got back and there was barely any space to lie down. Afraid of tripping over somebody in the dark, Roza squeezed herself into her usual spot behind the door.

She was almost asleep when the sound reached her ears. Eerie, like someone playing music underwater.

Slowly it came to her. She sat up, properly awake now. It wasn't the radio. It was her *phone*. Rusty must have put it on to charge ready for meeting his daughter. And it was throwing out the ringtone Jason had assigned himself when he gave it to her.

Chapter Thirty-Eight

KNOWING JASON WAS TRYING to contact her changed everything. She *hadn't* been abandoned. He might not have answered her SOS all those weeks ago but he must still care about her. Roza was gripped by a sudden desperate longing to see him. *Good morning, Miss Albania!*

Could he help them escape? Was that too much to hope for?

'I want to know more about Jason,' Hanna said, when Roza told her the next morning.

'He's funny. And cute.' Roza smiled. *His arm hooked around her neck. That first kiss.* 'Not like movie star cute or anything. He has freckles on his nose and his front teeth are snagged but when he smiles, his eyes dance.' *Had she really said that? It sounded so corny!*

'You really fancy him, I can tell.'

'He's generous too. When we went to London for the day, he paid for everything – even lunch in an Albanian restaurant.'

It had all begun so perfectly...

'He took me to the bandstand where his grandfather played the steel drums. Told me more about his family. That showed me his heart. How much they meant to him. After that...'

Roza's face folded. It was coming back to her now in full technicolour, how the day had ended. Then the horrible argument the next day in Wendy's garden. It was a long time since she'd given it any thought.

He'd only wanted to help.

Hanna was frowning. 'What?'

'The day after that, Jason and I had a big fight.'

'Didn't you kiss and make up?' Hanna tittered and made a silly kissy face.

Roza stood up. She had said too much. Only one thing mattered now. She had to find a way to make contact with him.

Vinny was a constant presence at the farm. There was no lounging in the easy chair or gambling on his phone now. He stood over them, checking the plants, telling them how much trouble they'd made for him with Dori. He couldn't go past either of them without issuing a tirade of abuse. Or stabbing them with a burning cigarette end whever he felt like it. Roza tried not to show her fear – it only made things worse. But Hanna cowered every time he came to check on them.

They needed to get a message to Jason. But how?

Roza counted the notches on the table. Eight long days had passed since his call. He might not guess her silence meant she was in trouble. What if he thought she was still upset about their quarrel? And even if she *could* make contact, how would he find her? As she reminded Hanna, they still had no idea where they were being held.

'You've been quiet all week.' Hanna looked up from the floor. She was taking breaks more often these days when Vinny wasn't around, dozing for longer under the lamps. 'You spend too much time thinking,' she said. 'Not good for your brain.'

Roza shrugged her shoulders.

Hanna yawned and stretched. 'Don't give up. You will think of something. I will try too. Have we finished watering for the day?'

'I think so. Vinny went off in a car with the Weasel so we won't see them for a while.'

'I thought of a game we can play,' said Hanna. 'It's called *Best*. I played it with the other girls when I was in hospital. Long hours there too. *Best food, best friend, best day* . . . I tell you; you tell me. And you have to give a reason.'

'A game?' Roza pulled a face. 'Later?'

'You need something to distract you now.' Hanna patted the floor next to her.

'OK, you go first,' Roza said without much enthusiasm. 'Best food?'

'That's easy for me. Fried meatballs. Mami's were the best, her own recipe, lots of oregano. Why? Because we always had them with fresh fries.'

Roza couldn't help smiling. 'You mean *French* fries.'

'Whatever. They still tasted good.'

'Pizza is my favourite,' Roza said. She told Hanna the story about the first time she'd tasted it at Mrs Cicu's.

'OK. Best day.' Hanna started telling her about the day her father turned up out of the blue and took her to the circus.

But Roza was already back in November, the 28th to be exact. The hundredth anniversary of their country's freedom from Turkey. Mrs Cicu had been teaching the history class about it all term. The whole country was decked out in red and black. There wasn't a single house in their village where the double-headed eagle flag wasn't flying or draped out of an upstairs window.

Roza was up early that morning helping Mami prepare food for the street party and trying to keep Ylli clean. She could picture Babi now in traditional clothing that included his *qeleshe*, the white brimless hat handed down to him by his grandfather. Lorik and his friends were there, sneaking glasses of raki when Babi wasn't looking.

In the evening, they climbed to the village high point with their neighbours to watch the firework display down the coast. Everyone joined hands as the sky exploded with light.

'Our last happy day together,' Roza said softly.

'Are you sure you don't have any idea where this place is?' Roza said the next morning. On Mug's instructions, they had been topping up the pots with extra soil and adding special plant food.

Hanna was on the floor. She had done her share of the work. Now, after another bout of coughing, she was concentrating on slow, deep breathing.

Roza shifted the half-empty bag of compost to the last table and went to wash her hands. Pressing Hanna for road names wasn't going to get them out any faster. But they needed to get a message to the outside soon. If they couldn't, Roza wasn't sure Hanna would make it out alive.

Chapter Thirty-Nine

Roza's first sight the next morning was Rusty's hairy legs filling the doorway. Vinny was behind him, Tamara too, swinging her truncheon.

'On your feet. Come on, you lot. Time to go to work. Christmas is coming – season of goodwill and all that.'

It was the third time that week Rusty had come looking for girls to beg on the streets. So far, she and Hanna had avoided being picked.

Rusty stepped forward. 'And it's a Sunday. The God botherers will dig even deeper when they see how pathetic you lot look.'

'We weren't back till three.' Wiping the sleep from her eyes, a girl with a tattoo that covered most of her chest sat up.

Rusty strode across the floor, grabbed a handful of the girl's hair and yanked her to her feet. 'You telling me my job, bitch?'

The girl shrieked and tried to pull away.

'Anyone else want to have their say?'

Rusty let her go. His eyes landed on Hanna. 'You're coming too, Snakeface.

Time you did some proper work.'

As Hanna pushed herself up to sitting, Roza braced herself, terrified she would make a fuss and there would be more violence.

'Take me instead,' she said quickly. 'You know I can do a better job than *her*.' She feigned a sneer.

Rusty threw his head back and laughed. 'Tell you what. You can both come. Two for the price of one!'

The girls selected were taken downstairs. Tamara dumped a pile of clothes on the floor – long skirts and headscarves in a dirty grey to put on over what they were wearing and make them look more like refugees. When the headscarves ran out, Tamara went looking for a substitute for Hanna.

'I have an idea,' Hanna whispered. 'Sometimes there are opportunities . . . you know, to run.'

No, No! Roza touched Hanna's arm and locked eyes with her. Her eyes were bright – too bright. Her skin hot to the touch.

Tamara was back. 'Use this.' She tossed a white towel at Hanna.

'She's sick. She shouldn't be going,' Roza said.

Tamara ran her eyes over Hanna and shrugged. 'She can stand, she can work.'

Outside, the Weasel and a man Roza hadn't seen before were smoking together beside two dark blue vans. The lettering on one of them had been painted over but a big white tick was still visible.

Vinny directed Roza and Hanna and two others into the first vehicle. Rusty got in next to the driver. Another four girls had gone off with Tamara.

Roza found herself on a long bench next to Hanna. At least they hadn't been split up. She tried to catch her eye.

'Mos bëj asgjë idiote,' she mouthed. *Don't do anything stupid.*

Vinny climbed in the back with the girls. As he handed out hoods, the van moved slowly down the track to the main road.

Rusty turned around from the front. They would each be directed to their allocated pitch, he told them. They were to kneel on the ground, holding out a begging bowl. All of them.

When the van was parked, Vinny gave them signs to hold up.

Roza read hers: *I don't speak English. Please support me and my sick baby.* Underneath the text, a photo of a crying newborn.

'No funny business now.' Rusty disappeared from the front seat to yank the back door open. He scanned them each in turn as they clambered out. 'Don't think we won't be able to see you, because we will. All the time.'

They were parked on an empty patch of ground next to a building site. There was a couple with a dog strolling along a path on the far side. Otherwise, it was quiet.

'You're with me, girlie.' Vinny seized the arm of the girl with the chest tattoo. 'You too, Snakeface.'

Hanna and Roza's eyes met as he led them away.

Rusty gave instructions to the driver and walked round to where Roza was waiting with the fourth girl. 'And you,' he growled into her ear, 'don't even think about making any trouble. Just remember, I got my spade ready to dig that hole anytime, night or day.'

He directed Roza to a pitch on the intersection of the high street and another main road. She recognised the names of some of the big stores that she'd seen in Thornley. A constant tide of people flowed to and from the train station at the foot of the hill.

She settled on an empty spot against a wall and bunched her skirt up into a cushion for her knees. Beyond the crossing, Rusty leaned against a postbox, eyes flicking up and down the street as he talked on his phone.

She had given the beggars in Thornley a wide berth. Now she understood what it was like to feel invisible. One or two passers-by glanced down at her as they tossed a coin or two in her bowl. Most kept their eyes fixed straight ahead.

The morning wore on. Roza's hunger pains were always worse in the middle of the day. Sunshine streamed between the clouds but the wind was icy. And her back was aching. She sat with her legs crossed, letting her body flop forward for a few minutes, knowing Rusty would make her pay for it later.

She looked around hoping to see Hanna. She couldn't be far away.

'Oh, you poor thing. You must be frozen. Let me get you a coffee and a sandwich.' A girl with rainbow pigtails and small round glasses was standing over her. She wore stripy fingerless gloves and the tattoos decorating the backs of her fingers and thumb spelled out the word J-E-S-U-S. Roza twisted round on to her knees.

The girl's eyebrows drew together as she read the card. 'You don't speak English? I'll get you a pouch of baby food as well.'

Please, help me. The words were forming on Roza's lips when Rusty's face appeared in her eye line.

A sudden flurry of noise made Roza turn. It was coming from down the hill but too many heads were in the way for her to see properly. She scrambled to her feet and looked up for Rusty. He had disappeared.

It took Roza a minute to make the connections. The figure with flailing arms running full pelt. The policeman at the opposite end of the station steps. Rusty's red hair flying like a cock's comb in the wind.

The screams for help didn't even sound like Hanna. She had lifted up her skirt and the white towel was unravelling down her back. The dark blue van with the tick on the side was in a line of cars leaving the station, moving slowly but steadily towards her. The traffic cleared and the van gained speed.

What was Hanna doing? She'd never reach the policeman in time.

Rusty jogged alongside the van as it slowed to a halt. Moments later, it pulled away with a screech of tyres and disappeared into the traffic. Hanna was nowhere to be seen.

A small crowd had formed. One woman had picked up the towel, another was crying and pointing up the road.

The policeman hurried over to the little crowd, a walkie-talkie angled against his mouth.

The rainbow girl was strolling towards Roza carrying a styrofoam cup; a paper bag over her wrist.

Roza felt a hard squeeze under her elbow.

'Not a peep from you, girlie. Time to go.'

Vinny propelled Roza in the opposite direction. His hand shook under her arm and there was a sheen of sweat on his upper lip.

Tamara was waiting with her four girls outside a block of flats. The road was a dead end. No one was going to make a run for it here. Vinny's grip loosened.

'What has Rusty done with Hanna?' demanded Roza.

Vinny dragged her to a wire fence out of sight of the road. He drew his fist back and punched her hard on the face. 'Shut up. Just shut up or there'll be more of that when we get back.'

Roza cried out and clutched her cheek. It was crackling with pain and one of her teeth had come loose. Thinking she might pass out, she sank on to a low wall and dropped her head between her knees.

Vinny's phone rang. 'What d'you mean, stuck in a ditch? You'd better get unstuck, you stupid Welsh sod.'

Roza looked across. It sounded like Rusty had plenty to say back at him.

'Listen to me.' The veins were standing out in Vinny's neck. 'This is all your bloody fault. Wait till Her Majesty finds out the mess you've got us into. What the hell were you thinkin'?'

He was talking about Hanna. Was she still in the van? Or had Rusty dropped her in a ditch somewhere, beaten black and blue? Roza could hardly bear to think about it.

Vinny lit a cigarette. 'Whatever happens, Dori's made it clear.' He turned for a

second to look at her.

What had Dori made clear?

'First thing tomorrow, the farm horses – they're bein' moved on. You got that?'

He was talking about her and Hanna.

Chapter Forty

INSTEAD OF TAKING ROZA back to the holding house as she expected, Vinny let her in to the farm and left. He wouldn't even look at her.

Roza threw her headscarf on to the floor, sat as close to one of the lamps as she could and hugged her arms around her waist. Even her teeth were chattering. She had never been more afraid.

Her sleep was interrupted by the whining sound of a car outside.

She dragged herself to the window, flattened herself against the wall and glanced down. It was the same car as the week before, parked up tight against the side of the house.

And two people again. One was definitely a man. He was pointing up at the farm although it was too dark to see his face.

The front door rattled. It could be the police, in an unmarked car, making enquiries about the incident involving Hanna. Or perhaps they'd been tipped off about the cannabis plants?

There was another possibility. It was someone with a grudge against Dori, like Hanna said.

She raced downstairs to attract their attention but the car drove off at speed. As Roza slammed her hands against the window, the front door flew open and Rusty tossed Hanna in like a bag of rubbish.

***

She was barely conscious. Roza slung the girl's arm around her neck and dragged her up to the farm. She laid her on the floor and covered her over with the long skirt. Her arms and legs were cold and stiff and when Roza tried to check her injuries, she moaned and curled into a ball.

Roza stood back, biting her lip. Babi used to reassure her about Lorik's asthma. As long as he could inhale it was OK. She watched the rise and fall of Hanna's chest. It didn't seem any worse.

She settled herself against the wall and drew her knees up to her chest. She would stay there all night if need be. And pray. It was all she could do.

She spent the next few hours dozing, sitting up with a start whenever Hanna moaned or shifted in her sleep. Now light was leaking into the sky. Roza dipped an ear towards to the girl's mouth. Her breathing wasn't silent but at least it had steadied.

Roza watched her for a few minutes more before getting up to stretch. Her back was stiff and sore. She walked round to the front room and flopped into Vinny's chair.

The blind had been left up and bright sunlight pressed in, warming the room. It must be well after eight. Vinny and Rusty would be coming for them soon.

The view across London was clearer than she could ever remember. Buildings, ancient and modern, wide stretches of green. And the River Thames – she couldn't see it, but that was out there somewhere, snaking its way through the city.

Today there was something else too. Something she hadn't noticed before. She stepped up to the window. A structure like an upturned table with four huge chimneys as the legs. If she'd ever found a way to speak to Jason that was how she would have described it. He'd lived most of his life in London. It might have meant something to him.

Was he still waiting to hear from her? Wondering why she hadn't got back to him? Too late to worry about that now.

Roza went to wake Hanna.

One of her eyes was half-closed with bruising. Congealed blood matted her hair above one ear. And those were just the injuries Roza *could* see.

Hanna whimpered as Roza helped her sit up to sip a mug of water.

'Are you hurt anywhere else?'

Hanna lifted her tee shirt to reveal a dark red footprint across her back.

Roza gasped.

'I curled into a ball but he carried on kicking.'

Roza ran the tap with warm water and used the corner of the headscarf to bathe the wounds on Hanna's face. She eased the tips of her fingers through the bloody knots in her hair.

Hanna drew a juddering breath. 'The policeman was too far away. Before I could get to him . . .'

A sob made her words inaudible. Roza sat limply beside her and waited.

'I wanted to conquer my fear, you see. To stop them having that power over me.'

'Oh, Hanna.'

The girl gulped at the air. 'But on the way back . . .' She clasped Roza's hand, her eyes shining through her tears. 'I saw it, Roza. The name of the road. I know where we are.'

The driver had turned too sharply just before the pothole track and the van had ended up in a ditch. 'I was thrown against the window. They were too busy nursing their own cuts and bruises to see me lift my hood.'

Roza forced a smile back at her. None of it mattered any more. Hanna didn't know it but in a short while Rusty or Vinny would be coming to kill them. And there was nothing they could do.

Chapter Forty-One

Roza's heart leaped into her throat as the front door opened with a crash.

'Where are you, you bastard?' yelled Rusty.

Vinny didn't move. He had been at the farm for an hour already, sitting on the edge of a table, swinging one leg, scrolling through his phone as though it was a day like any other.

Roza lowered her watering can to the floor where Hanna was sitting. They traded nervous glances.

'Talking to yourself again, Rust?' called Vinny.

Rusty appeared in the doorway, panting, his face dark with rage. He planted himself in front of Vinny. 'You snitched on me to Dori. Like I'm some kid in short trousers.' He thrust his face forward. 'Threatened me, she did. With a visit from those Albanian heavies she brings in for the really nasty stuff.' Spit sprayed from his mouth on to Vinny's face.

Vinny wiped his cheek with the back of his hand and sidled past Rusty on to

the landing. 'Nothing more than you deserve,' he snarled.

Rusty whirled round and, lifting Vinny up by his tracksuit collar, hurled him backwards across the landing. Vinny hit the wall with a thud. He stayed there for a moment then staggered to his feet. Shaking himself like a wet dog, he pulled his phone out and muttered something about showing Dori.

He was really going to film this?

Before he could start filming, Rusty came at him again. He drove his shoulder into Vinny's chest sending his phone flying. It skidded across the floor and landed at Roza's feet.

She stared at it. Any second, one of them would notice and pick it up. But it stayed there as Vinny launched himself across the floor with a roar. Grappling Rusty's leg he sank his teeth into his bare flesh. The Welshman roared with pain. With legs and fists flailing, the two of them wrestled across the floor towards the stairs.

Roza snatched the phone up. Then, slipping the farm key out of the lock, she fled inside and locked the door behind her.

She grasped Hanna's hand and spoke firmly. 'Quick as you can, behind the back tables.'

She brought up the phone keypad. Three bars – not brilliant, but it would have to do. Mumbling Jason's number to herself – she'd been rehearsing it in her head for weeks – she pressed the keys carefully.

'Who's this?'

He'd picked up! Roza let out the breath she'd been holding. 'Jason, it's me!

Dori's men caught me. I'm in London.'

Her words burbled out in a rush – a brief description of the potholed road, the position of the cannabis house, the upside-down table. Had she covered everything?

'It's off Blackbrook Lane. SW11.' Hanna gripped Roza's arm. 'Don't forget that.'

The low grunts that told her the men were still fighting had stopped. In its place a noise like a roll of thunder followed by an earsplitting shriek.

Hanna said matter-of-factly, 'I think one of them has fallen down the stairs.'

Roza tried to concentrate. Jason was still talking. 'Ro . . . it's gonna . . . OK . . . I text Mich—'

Michael. Was that what Jason was trying to say? *Michael Monette?*

Someone was rattling the door handle. Vinny was yelling, 'One of you bitches got my phone?'

Jason was gone. The signal had completely disappeared.

Roza tucked the phone inside her bra and eased Hanna gently to her feet. The door finally gave way with a resounding crack.

'Where is it?' Blood was oozing from Vinny's nose; his mouth set in an ugly line.

Mustering all her strength, Roza climbed on to the nearest table. There was no time to erase Jason's number. The sooner she could get rid of the phone the better.

She picked up one of the pots and flung it at Vinny, hitting him full in the face. He spluttered and wiped the earth from his mouth.

Three tables stood between Roza and the exit. She hopped her way across, kicking plants out of the way.

When she jumped down, Vinny made a grab for her shoulder. 'Come here you . . .'

She ducked under his arm. She could make it to the bathroom. Her foot skidded on a patch of something that looked like blood and she threw her arms out to steady herself.

The bathroom door was open. Vinny made a grab for her legs. But by the time he reached her, Roza had pitched his mobile into the toilet and pulled the flush.

He seized her by the hood of her sweatshirt and hauled her backwards.

'What is going on here?'

Dori! They hadn't heard her arriving.

Rusty, at the foot of the stairs now, was snorting like a racehorse, crouched forward, cradling the side of his head.

'So, you boys have been wasting time brawling instead of carrying out my orders?' Dori glowered down at him. 'The police are closing in thanks to you, Rusty. We need to clear the site. Now!' Her voice cracked like a pistol. 'Get on your feet! Prepare to move the cargo out. And keep your fists under control this time.' She checked her phone. 'I'm going back to the holding house. I'm expecting a call any minute confirming the new premises.'

She turned to face Vinny. 'Got hold of your phone, did she? Then the sooner we get rid of those two the better. You know what to do.' Her eyes slid across to Roza. 'You can't say I didn't warn you.'

As Vinny dragged Hanna into the hole, Roza sagged back against the spindles of the landing banister. With all that effort getting Vinny's phone, what had they achieved? She had no idea how much Jason had heard. *Upside-down table. Stupid description.* He wouldn't know what she was on about. Even if he'd made any sense of her words, the chances of him getting here in time were slim.

She paused to listen for a moment. Hanna wasn't even humming.

A car pulled up outside. Probably another guard arriving to help Vinny kill them – with a vehicle to drive them somewhere away from the house. The river? It couldn't be far away.

There was a thump on the door.

Standing over her, Vinny growled. 'Can't any of them remember the bleedin' code?' He pulled a cord from his pocket and, wrenching Roza's arms behind her, tied her to the banister spindles.

Another thump. 'A'right, a'right, I'm coming.'

Roza shut her eyes. Maybe she could outwit them as they tried to shove them into the car. Dodging past Vinny again wouldn't be a problem. There were plenty of bushes and undergrowth to give her cover at the back.

Who was she fooling? Here or somewhere else, she would die tonight. She and Hanna were done for.

Vinny was taking his time at the door, but she was tied too tightly to twist round and look down the stairs to see what was happening.

She definitely wasn't prepared for what happened next.

Vinny's cry of surprise. The oomph of someone's fist driving into his stomach. Then the steady click-clack of spiky heels on the stairs.

Blood pounded in Roza's head. *No, that wasn't right. It couldn't be.*

Chapter Forty-Two

Roza couldn't take her eyes off Adelina. Her black stiletto boots, the twitch in her left cheek. She didn't look good. Her eyes were puffy, the creases round her mouth deeper.

And Toska was with her. Hanna was right, Dori must have sacked him. Now he was working for *Adelina*. The car, the figures checking out the house – it had been *them*.

'What are you doing here?' There was no way Roza could disguise the tremor in her voice.

Adelina clasped her hands and raised a sneering mouth to Roza. 'Did you think you could run away and I would just let you go? Months of work Dori Dedja has had from you without paying me a penny. You are still *my* property and you will go wherever I decide. Your *Aunty Sade* . . .' Adelina spat out the words like they were arsenic on her tongue '. . . wanted you to have the very opportunities she denied me.'

'Denied? You were the ones with all the money and the maids and the big house . . .'

'*Don't be too harsh on her.*' Adelina mimicked her mother's voice. '*She's a bright girl. Reminds me of you at the same age. She might just be the one to get my brother's family back on its feet.*'

Sade was still evil. She'd tricked Hanna into leaving her village. And she must have known what Adelina was like and the grudge she nursed against Babi.

Roza strained as far forward as the cords would let her. 'Your mother uses her strength to prey on innocent people. And you. You are just as depraved as she is!'

'Revenge is a dish best served cold, isn't that what they say? Well, I have had twenty years to plan mine,' Adelina roared back. 'Her precious brother. Your Babi. *Frikacak!* Coward! Leaving my father to drown. I was clever *too*, the top of *my* class, but I had to leave school and work in a sausage factory. Can you imagine the shame? Now my mother thinks I cannot manage my own home or bring a filthy little witch like you into line.'

She hawked and spat on the floor.

Toska had been standing in the half-light at the far end of the landing. He untied Roza. 'We need to get the business done up here,' he said. 'Take her down to the car.'

'You have brought the diesel?'

'Wh-what are you going to do?' Roza stuttered.

'Go, woman! If you want this done, we must be quick.'

Toska kicked the farm door open and shook the contents of a metal can over the tables. They were going to set fire to Dori's precious plants. Adelina's way of getting even.

Roza screamed. 'You can't do that. There is a girl locked in the cupboard.'

Ignoring her, Adelina wrenched her arm behind her back and forced her down the stairs.

Just outside, Vinny lay unconscious.

Soft flakes of snow were flying into their faces. As Adelina raised a hand to shield her eyes, her grip loosened.

You're not as strong as you used to be Madam. Roza looked for a space to run. She slammed both hands into Adelina's chest then, head down, she charged forward. There was no way the woman would be able to catch up with her in those heels.

Roza swung sharp right and came face to face with Toska. He flipped her over his shoulder. She kicked with all her might but it was like attacking a slab of concrete.

'Is it done?' Adelina caught them up and steadied herself against a drainpipe,

'Burning nicely.' Toska smiled grimly. 'We both get to settle our scores.'

A low clunk followed and the trunk of the car sprang open. Roza was staring into the empty black space and bracing herself when the alarm started pulsating and the car lights blazed.

'You fool,' snapped Adelina.

As Toska fumbled with his key, Roza saw a figure in black flit into the bushes. A figure in a beanie!

She bit Toska's ear. He let out a shout and dropped Roza on to the gravel.

Pain shot down her spine. She rolled on to her front. Seconds was all she had before Toska seized her. Hoisting herself on to her hands and knees she crawled towards the bushes. Spiky leaves snagged on her sweatshirt as the alarm continued, sending out pulsing beams of light.

Keep going. Don't look back.

'Over here! Ro!'

Jason reached out for her. With one final effort she launched herself forward and let her body sag against his. Together they rolled down a bumpy slope and into a ditch.

An arc of torchlight swept the bushes. Roza lay rigid and held her breath.

Adelina's breathless voice spoke above them. 'She will go to the police. We have to find her!'

'And you are going to crawl around in those shoes, are you? You're out of your mind woman. Get in the car, the fire will soon attract attention. We are done here.'

Adelina let out a scream of rage. 'This is not over!'

Chapter Forty-Three

ROZA STRUGGLED TO HER feet. There was a lump the size of an egg on her forehead and she was trembling from head to toe. But she was alive. And the lights from Toska's car were no more than pinpricks in the distance.

'The fire! Jason, we have to get my friend out! She's locked inside a cupboard.' They ran towards the open front door.

Jason sniffed the air. 'Diesel. Petrol would've already exploded.'

'Quick then,' said Roza.

He shone a light on Vinny. 'He could come round any minute and call a couple of heavies.'

Roza glanced across to the holding house. *Top priority*, Dori had said. *Moving the cargo out*. So why were there no lights? No sign of any activity?

'I'll call the fire brigade.' Jason already had his phone out. 'The police'll be here . . .'

But Roza wasn't listening. She tore up the stairs with Jason close behind. She had assumed smoke would be curling under the farm door by now, but the air was surprisingly clear.

'Fire in there?' Jason pointed to the farm. The heat on the landing was intense. 'Lucky. Must be a fire door.'

'Hanna's in here,' Roza said.

Jason stood sideways on, ready to ram the door.

'No! It's really shallow. She'll be right behind it.'

Jason lifted his hands. 'Unless you know the key code . . .?'

Roza spun round. 'I think I do. What's the date?'

Jason screwed up his face. 'The 1st, I think.'

'Of what?'

'December.'

'If 3110 was good for October . . .' Roza bit her lip, concentrating. 'Try 3112.'

At once, the door gave way and Hanna slumped forward with a moan.

'Hi Hanna, nice to meet you,' Jason said. 'C'mon, we need to get you out of here.'

No sooner were the words out of his mouth than the front door slammed shut. A shaft of air shot up the stairs. The farm door swung back with a crash. Hanna yelped. Tongues of flame were shooting through the bannister, blocking the staircase.

Roza shrank back as a scorching wave of heat hit her. 'We'll never get out that way now.'

'They've spilled fuel on the stairs too,' said Jason. 'Look how quickly it's caught.'

Jason pulled his roll neck up to cover his mouth. He bent down and lifted Hanna from the floor. 'We have to find another exit . . . and shut the door behind us.'

'No exit,' Hanna croaked before she was overcome by a coughing fit.

'Yes, yes there is!' With sudden clarity Roza could see it in her mind's eye. 'There's a bit that juts out on the ground floor, a garage or something. With a flat roof. I saw it when we first arrived. If we can get into the room above it, we should be able to jump from the window.'

'The garage is on that corner.' Jason pointed towards Vinny's room.

Roza stumbled towards it. Everywhere, there was the crackle and pop of wood being devoured by fire.

She threw herself against the side window. The shape of the flat roof below was just visible. 'Yes, yes, in here,' she shouted, giving a double thumbs-up.

Jason lowered Hanna on to the floor by the window and propped her up against the wall.

She was in a bad way; worse than Roza had ever seen her. And no wonder. The smoke was making it hard for all of them to breathe. But Hanna... she was leaning forward now, the muscles under her ribs sucking in with each laboured breath.

'Hang in there, Hanna,' Roza said, but the girl didn't look up.

Jason checked that the door was properly shut and joined her at the window. 'It looks a long way down.'

And the roof was narrower than Roza had thought. Jump too far out and they could miss it. She fumbled with the window catch. Of course, it was locked. She banged it in frustration. 'We need something to smash it.'

They both looked at Vinny's chair.

Jason picked it up and slammed it hard against the window. A spider's web of splinters spread across the glass.

Seconds later, there was a roar from the landing. Wisps of smoke appeared under the door. The fire had eaten up everything in its path and now it was coming for them. She didn't even hear Jason's second strike.

Fresh air blasted through the hole that opened up.

'Jason!'

Blood was running down his arm and on to the floor.

Roza yanked his coat from his shoulders and making a fist inside the sleeve she punched out the remaining pieces of glass. 'Press it tight against your arm,' she said. 'It'll help stem the bleeding.'

She leaned out of the window and squinted down. Snowflakes swirled around. And there was the off-key wail of a fire engine, sounding closer with every second that passed.

'Still think you can jump?' Jason said.

Roza nodded firmly. She levered herself up on to the windowsill. 'Whoa!'

That was narrow too.

Jason reached up to steady her. 'Bend your knees, then roll when you land,' he said. 'Less chance you'll injure yourself.'

The blood from his arm trickled down her leg. The drop was a good three metres, further than she'd expected. And now she was looking down, it was a far smaller space than she'd pictured and covered with a thickening mantle of snow.

A surge of something she couldn't put a name to stirred inside her. Determination? Hope?

She saw herself standing now before Adelina – taller somehow and unafraid. Her own voice strong and clear in her head.

You have no control over me any longer. I am Roza Noli and I am going to walk away from here, free to live my life in my own way.

Knives stabbed her feet as she hit the ground. She slumped on to her side and rolled into the snow.

When she tried to sit up, a booming voice reached her ears. 'Anyone else up there?'

Roza struggled on to her knees. Figures in padded suits and helmets swarmed the ground below, setting up hoses to douse the flames. 'My friend Jason,' she shouted back. 'And a girl with asthma. Hurry please, she's very weak.'

'OK, let's get you on to terra firma.' The fireman's eyes were just discernible above his mask. She let him help her on to the rungs of the ladder. A few seconds later, she was on the ground, looking up to the house. She shielded her eyes, dazzled by the snow and the bright lights.

By the time she was wrapped up in the silver thermal blanket and taking small sips of water, Jason was halfway down. The firefighter settled him alongside her.

'You took your time,' she said shakily. If she didn't make a joke of it, she'd fall apart. Hanna. Adelina. Jason coming for her. The fire. She just couldn't take it all in.

'I couldn't jump.' Jason looked embarrassed. 'I've always been afraid of
heights.'

'Nasty gash on your arm, mate,' said the man who seemed to be in charge. 'The paramedics will put something on that now before we get you checked out. You've both had a lucky escape. And your friend . . .' He nodded towards Hanna who was being stretchered into an ambulance. 'Her breathing's bad. But she's in good hands.' He ran a hand over his face. 'What were you doing up there anyway?'

'Thank you, Station Officer. I'll take it from here.'

A woman in a belted coat and boots flashed an ID card. 'DI Sonya Smart. Modern Slavery Human Trafficking Unit.'

'You're not taking her anywhere.' Jason attempted to stand up.

'It's all right. Really. Nothing to be alarmed about.'

There was a man with her. His greying hair was peppered with snowflakes and he had the longest legs Roza had ever seen. Something about his face seemed familiar.

His eyes rested briefly on Jason. Then he hunkered down beside Roza and extended his right hand. 'Roza Noli? I'm so very pleased to meet you at last. I'm Michael Monette.'

Chapter Forty-Four

THE SOFT TAP ON the door stirred her. She opened her eyes to find bright sun streaming between the curtains.

'OK to come in?' Jason looked unsure.

Roza pulled herself into a sitting position and drew the duvet cover over her borrowed pyjama top.

'What time is it?' She smothered a yawn. She must have gone back to sleep. Again.

'Just after ten. Juliana said it was OK to come around today.'

He transferred the tray of half-eaten porridge and toast on to the carpet and hovered next to the bed.

'You can sit down.'

Roza could see him properly now for the first time. The curls over his collar had disappeared, a line of stubble was sprouting around his chin and he was wearing a black leather jacket and jeans that looked like they were the right size for him for once. He seemed older, more responsible-looking.

She yawned again. 'Sorry. I think I could sleep all day.'

'How are you?'

'My head still hurts, and the bruises on my back . . .'

'Where that thug dropped you.' Jason leaned forward and slid his fingers between hers. 'And so thin, look at you Ro. In that ditch, I could feel all your ribs.' He shook his head. 'Working in a cannabis farm. It's wild! I thought I might never see you again, Miss Albania.'

Roza attempted a smile. At least that didn't hurt. 'The police rescued the other girls who were there. Did you know that?'

Jason nodded. 'There was a big report in the news.'

He brought it up on his phone.

'*The trafficking ring is thought to be part of a large syndicate operating between the UK and Albania. The London head of the ring is still believed to be at large.*'

Roza looked at him blankly. 'Dori? She's still out there?'

Jason leaned forward and stroked her cheek. 'The police will catch her.'

She shook herself. 'What day is it?'

'Tuesday. The fire was Sunday.' He blinked a few times. 'My eyes are still burning.'

The fire. Roza could still taste the smoke. And smell melting plastic and burning plants.

'It's warm in here too.' Jason blew out his cheeks and took off his jacket.

There was a bandage on his arm and a jagged graze across his forehead she hadn't noticed before. 'I still can't believe you found us, Jason.' She bit down on her lip. She was determined not to cry!

'Yeah, regular hero me.' A flush crept across his cheeks. 'Hey, listen. For the record, your description of the old Battersea Power Station was ace. *An upside-down table with four legs.*' He chuckled. 'I'd never have thought of that. And you had the road name. Piece of cake then, getting the bus from Catford.' He leaned down to pick up a corner of toast and started chewing.

'You were already in London?'

'Yeah, staying with Greg. It was doing my head in, Ro. Not knowing where you were, what might have happened. When Michael emailed me . . .'

'Yes. How did that happen?'

'I looked him up online. He's a top guy, Ro.'

She nodded slowly. Michael *was* good and kind, just like her teacher had said. So was Juliana. She was just a leaner, long-legged version of Mrs Cicu.

'When I tracked Michael down, he said he hadn't heard from you. I guessed then that something had gone wrong. So I just kept ringing your phone.'

'After the way I spoke to you at Wendy's . . . then when you didn't answer my SOS text . . .'

'It didn't come through for days. I was in the Brecon Beacons doing a Duke of Edinburgh trek. There was no signal.'

So many misunderstandings.

Jason looked like he was thinking. 'I've made it sound like a bit of an adventure – Indiana Jones and all that. But honestly Ro, getting your call, all I could think was, this could be life or death. I've gotta get it right.' He tipped his head towards hers and cupped her face in his hands. 'It's OK, you're safe now. Cruella can't reach you. No way am I letting you out of my sight.'

Roza sank back into the pillows while Jason finished off the toast.

'Oh, I nearly forgot – Hanna's doing better.' He licked the jam off his fingers. 'But they're not likely to discharge her anytime soon. They need to get her asthma sorted.'

Roza excused herself to go to the bathroom. Going over everything with Jason, filling in all the gaps, it only made her think more about the things she *didn't* know. About her family. Sonya Smart was in touch with the police in Albania. The minute there was any news she would let Michael know.

Roza rehearsed the scene she had been holding in her head for so long. Walking into Babi's arms at Tirana. Searching his face. Unable to hold back any longer: *Babi, why did you sell me?*

Would they ever be able to get past everything that had happened?

And if the news wasn't what she was hoping for?

One way or another she was going to find out soon.

Roza peered up at the three-storey block of flats. There was no light in the entrance lobby, but between the faded lettering she could just make out the name. *Easton Court*.

Jason steered her past a pile of rubbish bags and the sour smell of rotting food. Somewhere above them, a dog howled.

'Top floor, sorry. There's no lift. Thank you, Catford Council! One of the reasons Mum had to move out. I can give you a backy if you like?'

The flat was tiny. She could see that straight away. Jason flashed the torch on his phone. 'No lights or heat either. But I've brought a few candles.'

He explained the layout. One bedroom and a small living room. Beyond it, a bathroom and a kitchen.

Roza blew her breath into her cupped hands as Jason placed the pizza box on the kitchen table.

A thought was niggling at the back of her head. He'd mentioned Catford on Tuesday. She punched his arm lightly. 'You've been to see your mother, haven't you? Why didn't you say?'

'I was gonna tell you tonight.' He pulled a knife from a drawer and cut the pizza into rough pieces. 'She can't move about much on her own yet, but . . .'

A full-beam-headlights grin filled his face. 'The staff at the home are great. And there's a group she's gonna join, supporting people with bereavement and stuff.'

'That's great. I'm so pleased for you . . . and her.' Roza gulped down a mouthful of water and coughed. 'Are those bits of chilli?'

She flapped her hand over her mouth and waited for the heat to die down. 'Is that why you brought me here, Jason? To tell me about your mother?'

He stared into the candlelight, poking the softening wax with his finger. 'Tell the truth, I haven't been able to stop thinking about the way our day in London ended. I wanted to see you on your own. Away from Michael and Juliana. Just us. Like it was that day in September.' He reached for her hand. 'Before everything went wrong.'

'Oh, Jason! And this is your idea of a romantic dinner for two?'

He gave a reluctant laugh.

She pushed the food away and rubbed her eyes. 'Sorry. It's crazy I'm so sleepy. I've only been up seven hours.'

'You'll get stronger. Come on. You can take a nap next door.'

A lamp post was casting a line of light across the bed. Jason drew the curtains and pulled back the duvet.

'I mustn't be late getting back to Woodside Park. Michael and Juliana will be back from their dinner. They'll worry if I'm not there.'

'It's only just after seven. Plenty of time yet.'

'What are *you* going to do?' Roza looked at the bed then up at him. Heat flooded her neck and face.

'OK if I stay here with you?' She felt him tense. 'Just to hold you, keep you warm. Nothing else, promise.'

She would never have suggested it. But at that moment she knew that was exactly what she wanted too.

'All right,' she said.

***

She must be dreaming. A phone was bleating and every time she tried to answer it, it moved out of reach. If she could only open her eyes.

The phone Juliana had given her was lit up, pulsing like a heartbeat. Roza eased herself out of Jason's arms, leaned forward and grabbed it. Her brain was in a fug. It was only just after nine.

'Roza! It's Michael. Are you OK?' His voice sounded urgent.

She cleared the sleep from her eyes and sat up properly. 'I'm with Jason. Are you home already?'

'No, we're leaving now. Roza.' He cleared his throat. There was a pause. 'I've just heard from Sonya Smart. About your family.'

Roza shivered. Like someone had opened a window and let in a gust of icy air.

'Tell me, Michael.'

'We'll pick you up from Jason's on the way home. Give me his—'

'No, Michael – now. Please! I have to know.'

Chapter Forty-Five

SHE LET THE PHONE drop on to the bed and stared into the dark.

Jason had pulled himself up beside her. His arm crept round her shoulder.

'Was he certain? That they all died?'

'There was a crash.' She closed her eyes, pushing away images she'd seen on TV of car accidents; bodies strewn across the road. 'The lorry driver - he died too. The road was closed. They were driving back from my grandmother's.'

Why was she giving him all these details? She had lost her family. Nothing else mattered.

'Did Michael say when?'

'21st September. The day we were in London. More than two months ago.'

All that time she'd been at the cannabis house plotting her escape, they had been lying under the earth. She'd never stopped hoping she would see them again. Now she knew for certain she never would.

'I just can't take it in, Jason. I was convinced the news delay from Tirana meant they were all still alive. I was ready to sit down and talk with Michael about the future. About going back. But now...'

Her shoulders shook as she gave way to tears. When she woke up tomorrow morning, it would still be true. And all the mornings after that.

Jason held her tight and she could feel his body shuddering too. He, of all people, would understand how she was feeling.

She pulled away from him and stood up, smoothing the creases in her top. 'Michael and Juliana will be here soon,' she said. Her insides felt tight – as if they were held together by wound-up elastic. If she let go, properly let go, she felt as though she would fall apart.

She sat down on the edge of the bed to tie her shoelaces. She would always remember where she was when she heard the news. She twisted round to look into Jason's face. 'Thank you for being here with me,' she said.

Michael's study was a gloomy space at the back of the house, filled with a grainy desk, floor-to-ceiling bookshelves and a surprisingly large red sofa. Roza sat down, letting the soft leather mould itself around her. Michael, still dressed in his suit, turned on the fire and moved around, switching on lamps. Juliana handed her a mug of hot chocolate and joined her on the sofa, curling her legs under her baby-bump.

Roza studied the photocopied sheet of paper Michael had given her. She recognised the name of the local newspaper at the top.

Five die in Durres-Tirana Highway auto crash – 21st September.

She read it quickly. Only a few lines and no gory details, thank goodness. The only thing to hope was that they had all died quickly, without pain. Her heart felt like it was splintering into a thousand pieces. She accepted a tissue and blew her nose.

'In the absence of any family member . . .' Michael ran his finger down a sheet of scribbled notes. 'Your father's employer – a Mr Viktor Miloti? – was asked to identify the bodies. The police have failed to trace your father's sister, er . . .' He consulted his notes again. 'Sadete Dragusha.' He looked up at Roza. 'It seems she has disappeared. The police think Tirana was where she ran the Albanian arm of the trafficking operation. As for the woman who heads it up, Dori Dedja, she's disappeared too. But there are warrants out for their arrests.'

Roza bit her lip. She had to voice the thought that had been troubling her. 'Are the police sure it was an accident? Aunty Sade might have arranged for the car they were driving to be tampered with, to have them deliberately killed. She was capable of such wickedness; I know that now. If I had accepted my fate, not made trouble for Adelina . . .'

Michael and Juliana exchanged glances.

'Oh Roza,' started Juliana.

Michael cut in, 'No! The lorry driver skidded on a patch of oil from a previous spillage, lost control and crossed the highway. There is no doubt about that.'

A pumping sound from his phone shattered the silence that followed. He stood up and excused himself to take the call.

Juliana picked up Roza's hand. 'You have been through such an ordeal. And now this. Sorry doesn't begin to express how sad Michael and I feel for you.'

'You have both been so kind.' Roza removed her hand. What was she supposed to do now? Everything she'd planned, saved for, thought about. It had all been for one purpose – to return home.

Michael's voice boomed from the kitchen. *Yes. Really? That's very good news.*

'I have been trying to get hold of Kamila.' Juliana began gathering up the empty mugs.

Roza had been tuned into Michael's conversation. 'Sorry?'

'Kamila. My sister?' When Roza looked blank she laughed. 'Mrs Cicu?'

Roza flushed. *Of course, she knew her teacher's name.*

'We wondered if she might know any more,' Juliana continued. 'And, of course, we wanted to let her know you are safe and here with us.'

'She guessed what would happen didn't she?'

'She has rung us every month for the past year asking if there was any news of you. But getting through to her now has been impossible. Lines down in the snow maybe.'

Michael burst back into the room. 'That was Sonya again. Jozif Braka turned himself in at an Oxford police station early this evening. He told them where they could find his wife. She in turn disclosed Toska's whereabouts. They've all been arrested.'

Chapter Forty-Six

ROZA SNUGGLED UP TO Jason on the small sofa in Juliana's den.

'I went to see Hanna yesterday.'

'Not on your own?' Jason pulled his head back.

'No! Juliana took me. Hanna is still thin like a stick but her eyes were brighter, you know? And her breathing, so much better. She said DI Smart is going to find her somewhere safe to live, away from London.'

'Will you stay in touch?'

'Oh yes, I think so.'

They had been through so much together.

'There's a train from Paddington at 3.20,' Jason said suddenly. 'I should get back today. Term finishes next week. The college have been great about the time I've missed but . . .'

He had to go, of course. He couldn't stay in London indefinitely. Neither could she. Juliana had told her she could stay as long as she liked. And Roza knew she meant it. But their new baby would be arriving in a few months.

If Roza was going to stay in the UK she would need to apply for *leave to remain*, find something useful to fill her days.

Jason squeezed her shoulder. 'You could come back to Thornley with me now Cruella and co are out of the picture. Spend Christmas at Wendy's with me and Mum?'

'How is she?' Jason had just come from visiting her.

'She can't wait to meet you.' He raised an eyebrow. 'You haven't answered my question.'

Roza gave her head a tiny shake. 'Sorry. I don't think I ever want to go back to Thornley.'

The silence between them lengthened. She stared at the lilies Juliana had arranged in a jug on the windowsill. Some of the petals were already wilting.

'Did you feel the same when your father died? Cheated, I mean?'

Jason said, 'You don't think like that at twelve. It's since we lost Grandad I've thought more about Dad – what I missed out on.'

She was so afraid he was going to come out with something she didn't want to hear, she burst out, 'And don't tell me this feeling will soon pass, because I know it won't.'

She felt Jason flinch before he said in a quiet voice, 'Tell me about your dad – what he was like. I spent all the time in Thornley thinking he was this terrible tyrant from the Middle Ages.'

That made her laugh. 'No, he wasn't like that at all. Babi was sensitive and intelligent – he loved reading. He loved his family too. The trouble was he wanted to please everybody, I see that now. My mother, his sister especially, and me. And he couldn't make things right for all of us.'

She saw Jason sneak a glance at the clock on the wall. They didn't have long before his train.

'I'll come back,' he said. 'The week after Christmas? Will you still be here?'

Roza shrugged. She didn't know where she'd be.

***

Michael waited for her by the station escalator. Roza looked back one last time for a glimpse of Jason but he had disappeared into the crowds.

'I have a favour to ask,' Michael said in a cheery voice. 'I need to choose a Christmas gift for my wife. A bit last minute, I'm afraid. Juliana finished her shopping weeks ago.'

Last minute? It was only the twelfth of December.

Michael insisted on a hot chocolate first. Roza sat politely waiting, willing him to look up from his phone and ask if she would prefer to go back to Woodside Park. There seemed no end to the number of messages he had to scroll through. Finally, he put the phone down and gave her a long look.

'You're tired. Juliana's present can wait. Let's head back.'

The light was fading fast, though the pavements still teemed with shoppers. The snow had given way to a hoar frost that clung to the trees and pavements. Decorations shimmered above the traffic. As they left Woodside Park station, a brass band was playing 'Silent Night'.

Roza pulled the collar of the coat Juliana had given her as high as it would go. Michael was humming under his breath. 'Juliana's favourite. Do you know this one, Roza?'

He stepped up his pace and she had trouble keeping up with his giant strides. When they arrived at the corner of their road, he stopped abruptly and pointed in the direction of their house.

What now? She was tired and not in the mood for playing guessing games.

Reluctantly she followed his finger beyond the red pillar box to their tiny front garden with its straggly hedge and half-open gate.

At first, all she could make out was Juliana standing tall, waving her arms over her head. Then Roza saw she was pointing at the person standing alongside her. Another woman, shorter and fuller, her dark hair pinned up in the way Roza remembered so well.

Mrs Cicu!

Roza broke into a run, her conviction growing with every step. Only when she reached the gate did she see *him* too. Longer and leggier than she remembered, and with an expression of total bewilderment on his face.

'Ylli!'

Roza stumbled up the steps, flinging herself against the two of them, calling their names over and over. Then Michael was there behind her and somehow they all crowded in through the front door – Juliana leading the way, Mrs Cicu with her arm around Roza's waist and Ylli wedged in the space between them.

The front room was alight with colour. Red and gold candles nestled between greenery on the mantelpiece. Paper lanterns hung from the ceiling and in the alcove stood a small fat Christmas tree topped with a star.

'They said my *whole* family.'

A huge sob tore through Roza's throat as they bunched up close together on the sofa. She covered Ylli's hand with her own. It was really him. She wasn't dreaming.

Her teacher's eyes glittered with her own tears. 'That was what they told Mr Miloti. But when he was asked to arrange the funerals there was no mention of Ylli. I drove straight to the hospital. One of the nurses who had been on duty on the day of the accident remembered a small child admitted around the same time. They didn't realise he was part of the same family. He was still on the children's ward.' Mrs Cicu smiled down at him. 'No serious injuries, only bruises and cuts. He was found in bushes at the side of the road.'

As Roza traced a faded line on Ylli's forehead he shrank back, burying his head into Mrs Cicu's neck.

Suddenly, she remembered something. Something she carried with her all the time. She reached into her pocket. 'Ylli, look. A little piece of you has been with me all this time.'

She held it out. The blanket corner was more ragged than ever. Meeting her eyes for the first time, Ylli took it and rubbed it against his cheek.

'Our phone line and internet has been down for a week but when Juliana told me you were here, I could not believe it,' said Mrs Cicu. 'I had almost given up hope. Straight away, I made arrangements for me and Ylli to fly to London. And here we are!'

'Ylli is living with you?'

Mrs Cicu clasped Roza's hand. 'Of course! Will you come back with us and let us be your family now?'

Chapter Forty-Seven

Albania: Four months later

THE ARTIST'S IMPRESSION OF Adelina in the witness box was a good likeness. Too good. Roza shuddered and shut down the link Michael had emailed her.

Couple jailed for child trafficking.

For now, that was all she needed to know.

More than a week had passed since the trial ended. Finally, she and Mrs Cicu were able to return to the village. Cruel to the last, Adelina had denied the charges, forcing Roza to give evidence by video link from Tirana.

'Adelina Braka will be in prison for a long time,' Michael said when they spoke later that day. 'Her husband's sentence will be somewhat lighter. But he will never work as a doctor again.'

Poor Albi, likely to end up in foster care. Roza even felt sorry for Skender.

'The neighbour claimed knowing all along *something wasn't right*. And as for the police...' Michael gave vent to an angry sigh. 'Until people are willing to recognise trafficking could be happening right under their noses, in their own neighbourhoods.'

His tone changed. 'Have you been to visit your family's graves yet, Roza?'

She hadn't. Kamila – as she now had just about got used to calling Mrs Cicu – had been trying to persuade her. But the prospect of seeing the lives of the people she had loved most in the world reduced to a few slabs of stone was more than she could bear.

Roza cleared her throat. Hanna had been in touch, she told him brightly. Living in Cardiff, in her own flat, and receiving proper treatment for her asthma. 'I'm still afraid Dori will go after her though,' she added.

'Sonya Smart assures me they'll continue looking for Dori Dedja. And, of course, the charges will include murder now.'

The girls who disappeared. The mounds of earth. That had come out during the trial too.

'And my aunt?'

'I'm told they're following up some useful leads but . . .'

'She could still be trafficking girls,' Roza interrupted. 'That's right, isn't it?'

Chapter Forty-Eight

SOON THEY WOULD BE moving away from the village. Safer for all of them, Michael said. Roza didn't think she would mind. There were too many memories there. No one would know where they were going. Although Jason would find out when he came to visit. He'd already booked his plane ticket for the end of term, a gift from Wendy

Roza was thinking of Babi and Mami now as she watched Ylli kicking a ball between the slide and the swing Mr Cicu had erected. They were slowly becoming good friends again, she and her little brother. She had been talking to him about the games they used to play, the stories she would read him, the places they went to together when he was a baby.

She looked up as Kamila, back from shopping, parked her car. She scuttled towards them, a brown paper package in her hands. Ylli's football came flying up the garden. When Roza failed to return it, he stamped his foot and ran inside.

'Mr Miloti was on his way here with this.' Kamila sounded breathless. She handed Roza the package, held together with a thick elastic band

He and Stefanie had already called to *pay their respects* before the court case. And to deliver a small box of her parents' personal possessions – her mother's wedding band, some tools belonging to Babi, a few books Roza recognised. It had been an awkward meeting. Mr Miloti had no small talk and Stefanie, who had never been lost for a word in her life, could only blink and stare, as though Roza had landed from another planet.

Roza sat down on the garden seat. 'Letters,' she said, pulling the paper away and looking up. 'From Babi.'

She flicked through the envelopes. They were all addressed to her at 44 Ridley Road. Stamped *RETURN TO SENDER.*

'Viktor said he found them yesterday when he was clearing out an old filing cabinet at the garage. He thinks your father must have kept them there to save your mother from finding them.'

Roza didn't understand. 'The post arrived every day. I never saw these.'

Kamila's dress rustled as she sat down in the space next to her. Roza heard her breath catch. 'Your cousin must have given the postal service instructions to return them unopened.'

'So he would know I never received them.'

Roza picked up the letter on top and pulled out a single sheet of paper dated 18th June the previous year. She spread the letter across her knees.

Vajza ime më e dashur (My dearest daughter)

Many months have passed and I do not know if you are ok or where you are. When I phoned your cousin, she said many bad things to me. Your Mami has cried and cried and my heart is heavy because I knew you were not being treated well. I owed many people money and your aunty had this plan to help me and, I believed, to help you too. Adelina would give me money so I could clear my debts and get treatment for your Mami.

I was a stupid man to believe what my sister said. I went to see her many times but she told me it was too late to

change the arrangement. She even said you were no longer my daughter because Adelina had paid for you. But I told her no, Roza Noli will always be my daughter and I want my daughter back.

Roza read it through and then once again. She handed it to Kamila.

'Your poor father,' Kamila said.

It was all Roza could think of. How desperate Babi must have been to turn back the clock and make things different. But with an overbearing sister, a sick wife and a family to provide for, what choice did he have? Roza understood that now. He must have hoped for the best for her but did not fear the worst until it was too late.

Later that night she crept into the room where Ylli was sleeping. His arms and legs were splayed out like a star. His slack thumb rested on his cheek. Roza's heart contracted. *How could a sister do that to her brother?*

Mrs Cicu found her dozing in the chair as bone-white light seeped into the room. Roza sat up and, with a suddenness that surprised them both, said, 'I think I would like to visit their graves.'

They drove through the still-sleeping village – Roza clutching a few spring flowers picked from the garden. There was no way to tell Babi that she forgave him. She was thankful just to know the truth now. That he loved her and fought for her. Laying flowers on his grave was her way of making peace between them.

She tried to push his anguish to the back of her mind. None of this was her fault and there was nothing she could have done to prevent it. Kamila kept reminding her of that.

'He never told me about the bad blood between him and Adelina,' Roza said, looking across at Kamila's profile. 'And there is no mention of it in any of his letters. I don't think he had any idea how bitterly she felt towards him.'

She would not go through her own life nursing the same ill will towards Adelina. She had made up her mind about that.

Holding on to anger only hurts our own hearts. That's what Kamila had said when they talked about it. Roza would never forget what Adelina had done to her – the scar above her eyebrow was a daily reminder – and she wasn't ready to forgive her. Not yet. But maybe in time . . .

The indicator clicked. Her teacher turned up a narrow section of road and pulled the car on to a dusty verge. 'They are just simple graves.' She reached into her bag. It was just light enough to see the letter she pulled out. 'Plot 917. Up here, I think.'

They found them quickly, in a short strip shaded by new saplings. Kamila crouched down to brush away dead leaves and clumps of earth. The stones were bare – no names or dates.

Roza laid the flowers and bowed her head. After a few moments, she looked up. The people she loved were not really here – in her heart she knew that – and she did not have to come here to remember them.

'When I am older, with money of my own, I will arrange a proper gravestone with their names,' she said.

They took the coast road home to avoid the morning traffic. The sky was a cloudless canopy, painted pink by the early morning sun.

Roza saw the *Sunrise* painting in her mind. The fishermen casting off in their little boat. The flickers of flame on the water. The hope of the day ahead.

Most children who were trafficked did not come back, yet she had been given another chance. Inside, she was not so very different from the girl who had flown to the UK twelve months before. She still cherished the same dreams and she was ready to start her new life, wherever that might be. For that was what it felt like – a new life.

She wound down the window. The air was salty on her tongue.

'Are you ready to go home now?' Kamila turned to look at her.

Roza smiled. She was ready.

Afterword

Thank you for reading this book. We hope you've enjoyed it!

Authors love hearing readers' thoughts about their books, so please leave a review on Goodreads or a site you used to buy this book.

If you're on X, you can also share your thoughts about *Sold* and tag Sue Barrow – @SueBarrow1.

Either way, other readers get to hear about the book.

Sign up for Sue's newsletter at **suebarrow.com**. You'll get news, book recommendations, special offers and a free copy of the article mentioned on page 253.

Sue is on Facebook as *Sue Barrow Children's Author*

Facts About Human Trafficking

'Human trafficking is the process of trapping people through the use of violence, deception or coercion and exploiting them for financial or personal gain.'
    Anti-Slavery International

Though Roza Noli is a fictional character, the circumstances in which she finds herself are all too real for the millions of young people caught up in human trafficking today. Some, like Roza, are sold by their families – tricked into sending them abroad on the promise of a better life. Others become caught up in different forms of modern slavery – kidnapped into the sex trade, forced to give up their kidneys for organ transplants or to work in cannabis farms or nail bars.

It is estimated that over forty million people across the globe are trapped in modern slavery – and one in four is a child. This figure includes adults and children who are trafficked *within* the UK, as well as those brought here illegally.

Thankfully, many charities are working across the globe to combat this evil trade.

International Justice Mission (IJM) is one of these. They work in partnership with law enforcement agencies, governments, survivors and communities to stop modern slavery, trafficking and violence in Europe and around the world.

As a Freedom Partner with IJM, I am donating a percentage of my royalties from this book towards their work. My book is published independently of IJM and is not based on their work or stories. But their impact inspires me and, by supporting them in this way, I hope that more people will be brought to safety from trafficking.

www.ijm.org

The National Referral Mechanism is the UK Government's system for supporting victims of modern slavery. If you want to record a concern or suspicion of slavery, or if you need advice or more information, you can call the Modern Slavery Helpline – **0800 0121 700.**

Or you can report it online.

About the Author

Sue Barrow has lived in Cardiff for most of her life. As well as writing contemporary fiction for teens, she is the author of local history books for children on Cardiff and the South Wales Valleys. Her large and growing family continues to provide inspiration for her stories.

Sue loves walking the Wales coastal path, eating shellfish and beating her family at board games.

Sold is her second novel.

Acknowledgements

The idea for writing *Sold* came to me after I read about a court case in the British press in 2008. A professional couple who smuggled a teenage girl into the UK had then forced her to work long hours unpaid – cooking, cleaning and caring for their child. She was also physically abused and denied schooling.

Child trafficking (domestic slavery in this case) was a crime I had never heard of and, talking to my own teenagers and their friends, I discovered I wasn't alone in my ignorance. Straight away, I knew this was a subject I had to write about. Within a few weeks I had mapped out a plot for a young adult novel.

Of course, I realised my story, any story, wasn't going to make even the tiniest dent in this appalling trade. But written as a thriller – exciting and engaging, well-researched and with respect to the culture portrayed – it might make people sit up and take notice. That was my goal.

Fourteen years later, as *Sold* has slowly edged its way to publication, I would like to thank:

God, for being there every step of the way.

Philip Lewis, for sponsoring *Sold*.

Imogen Cooper and her team at the Golden Egg Academy for teaching me the art of story writing for children . . . and making it so much fun!

Kathy Webb, my GEA mentor, for her wisdom, insight and guidance.

The good friends I've made among my fellow writers. Julie, Kurstyn, Amy (thanks for the nail polish idea!), Kiera, Jo and Rebecca – you have all been unstintingly supportive.

My beta readers – Lilia, Julie and Faith – who offered helpful suggestions, as well as spotting a few glitches.

Ethan Wayman, for putting me right on text speak.

My reading group – friends one and all – for their encouragement and book recommendations.

Dr David Gallacher for his expert guidance on the development of asthma symptoms.

Nikki Doci who helpfully answered my questions on Albania history, culture and family life.

Jennette Slade, for the remarkable cover design.

Gary Dalkin for his support during the editing process.

I owe Cadence Publishing a huge debt of gratitude for taking me on. And especially Sophie Beal, not only for all the hard work she poured into this, but for believing in my story and recognising its importance from the outset.

Finally, a heartfelt thank you to my family:

John – for the writing space; and space (and time and encouragement) to write.

Kate, Amy, Tom, Jo and Ellie and their spouses (especially Ian, my website designer) for their patience and unflagging interest.

Simon and Sara (and my dear late dad) for urging me on to the finishing line.

Thank you one and all!